THE NIGHT ALPHABET

DAVID M. DONACHIE

Published by **Solipsist Press 2018**
Edinburgh, Scotland

This is a work of fiction. Any similarity between the characters and situations within its pages and places or persons, living or dead, is unintentional and co-incidental.

ISBN: 978-1-9804-2532-8

To my wife, Victoria, who came up with half the ideas; to Kay Gillespie, who was already ready to read what I wrote, even when I kept changing things; and most of all to my Father, who filled me with the love of stories and the love of writing.

Also to Sparta, my dearly beloved cat, who died the day that this book was published.

CONTENTS

Introduction

I have always been something of an insomniac. In amongst the restless tossing and turning between going to bed and sleeping, my mind conjures up strange images, preposterous scenarios, and disturbing thoughts. Since I am also a writer, those images often suggest stories; ones with the most marvellous plots and intricate words.

By morning, the majority of those sleepless stories have vanished into the ether, and many of the rest prove to be a lot less enchanting to my waking mind than they were to my sleeping one – but not all. Sometimes the stories retain their magic, and their night-time mystery.

This collection is a product of those strange night time ideas, which is why you will find it full of nightmares, dreams, rain on windowpanes, storms, strange noises in the darkness, sleep, insomnia, and (quite literally) beds. You will also find the products of my wakeful imagination, and I hope you enjoy them both.

(I also like cats, ruins, and frogs, so you will find some of all of them as well)

David Donachie – 15th February 2018

A

… is for **Angels**

War in Heaven

I went to the window to watch the first of them arrive. They shuffled slowly down the street, heads bowed. There were only two or three of them, but I knew that a whole host was on its way – refugees in need of a home.

The day was sullen grey, limping under the burden of winter. The clouds bore down from above, but the strangers lit up the street like candles. The warm glow of them crept between my twitched aside curtains and made me think of spring, or of summer in the mountains. When I blinked, the light that bled through my eyelids was golden.

The street was almost empty. Only one man, his coat turned up under ginger hair, hurried past in the background, keeping his face firmly turned away from the refugees and their minders. He must have known that they were there. He must have felt the warmth of them through his gaberdine, but I suppose he did not want to see them. My neighbours, I was sure, were glued to the inside of their windows – just as I was to mine.

One of the minders stopped and pulled his charge aside. They were just below my window; they were walking towards the door; and I realised that this was to be the new occupant of the empty flat across the landing.

Just before he vanished from view the refugee looked up – his eyes were as golden as his hair. For a moment the wings at his back shivered, as if he could take to the air, and I thought that he had seen me; but then the head bowed, the wings drooped, and he vanished through the open door.

Angels. We knew that there had been a war, a terrible bitter struggle that had turned brother against brother. These refugees were the detritus of that war, fallen to earth with nothing but their tattered wings to shelter them. Some distant country had fed, and clothed, and worshipped them … at first. But the angels continued to fall – cold, and injured, and incapable of work – until the whole host had been moved on, shuffling their way across the continent until they wound up here.

I left the window and went to my door, determined to be more welcoming, but when the angel reached the top of the stairs, surrounded by a bluster of resettlement officers, I stood frozen with my hand on the doorknob and let them go by. I only got a glimpse of the angel, hemmed in as he was by men with checklists and women with forms. There was a brief interval of murmured conversation from behind the half closed door, and then the officials withdrew and left us alone.

For the longest time I remained at my door, expecting something to happen, but the little top landing stayed silent, growing slowly darker as the grey day became a charcoal dusk. When I pushed my door open a little wider I could see that the Angel had not even turned on the lights. There was only a faint golden glow behind the dirty glass above the door, and even that was fading.

Over the next few days I grew familiar with the proximity of the angel. He did not leave his flat, and no one came to visit, but I could hear him moving back and forth on the other side of the thin partition walls. He made a whispering sound, like the soft rustling of trees in the wind, and I realised that the tips of his wings were brushing against the wall. When I lay down in bed at night I imagined that I could see the angel's glow creeping across my bedroom ceiling.

When friends made excuses to call me on the phone, I told them that I had seen nothing, but this was not true. Once, returning early from work, I saw that the angel's door was open — I am not certain he even understood how doors worked. A section of the hallway was visible, and beyond it a small unfurnished room, pale with afternoon sunlight. The angel stood with his back to me. His wings were open, reaching from one side of the room to the other, and he balanced on his toes, as if at any moment he could take flight and return to the heaven he came from. His feet were bare, and dirty, and covered in scratches.

I am not sure why I lied. The angels were all anyone talked about in those days. I could have dined out on the story of having one for a neighbour, but something made me protective. Already I thought of him as *my* angel, and I wanted to hide him from a place that was already turning against his kind.

"I don't mind the ones we've got, of course," said the man who ran the corner shop as he rung up my milk and newspapers, "they keep to themselves. But there are so many of them. How are we expected to cope?"

The woman who sat across from me in the Doctor's waiting room said much the same to the friend who'd come with her for the toddlers' clinic. "They just aren't the same as us, know what I mean? They don't understand how to work, but they still get sick. I mean who's going to pay for that!"

"They aren't natural!" her friend agreed with relish. "I hear they haven't got anything, you know, down there!" She suppressed a gasp at her own daring, glancing around to make sure that the kids hadn't heard her.

"And those wings," she continued, "I heard they spread disease, like pigeons."

I wanted to interrupt. I wanted to tell them that the angels were beautiful, and that if they were not like us that was no crime, but I said nothing.

Later, outside, I saw that the same story about disease was printed in one of my newspapers. Only a month ago, it had lauded the government for finding the angels homes. Now it reported that whole flocks of them roosted together, surrounded by their own filth, in abandoned attics and warehouses. Not here, of course, but somewhere we could easily become.

"They ought to find someplace else for them to go."

A stranger's voice came unbidden from the other side of my raised newspaper. I lowered it cautiously, revealing a red-faced and red-haired man in a heavy coat.

"I'm sorry?"

He jabbed a finger at the front of my paper.

"Those creatures."

I folded down the corner of the paper, and saw that there was a picture of an angel on the cover – a striking image of a man wrapped in his own wings and cowering behind a cordon of police.

"They ought to take them away," he repeated with heavy emphasis, "somewhere else." With a start I realised that he was the same man that I had seen on the street the day the angels arrived.

"Have you met one?" I asked, mentally preparing myself to defend my angel at last.

"Oh yes," he said, and a queer look came into his narrow eyes that shut me up. "I know all about them. I've heard them. The noise they make. It sickens me."

I'd heard the angel too. Early in the morning and late at night, when the sun was rising and setting, he sang, like the birds do. It was a wordless song. Beautiful. Rising and falling away but never silent, as if the angel did not have to breathe. Some mornings I sat transfixed on the edge of my bed, listening to the song flow through the walls. It made me think of far away places that I had almost forgotten. It could not be the same sound that the stranger had heard.

I suppose that the angel must have heard something too.

A few days later he appeared on the landing dressed in conventional clothes: grey trousers, innocuous brogues, a hand-me-down jacket, and a shoved down hat. With his golden hair tucked back and his pale skin covered he looked almost human, but he couldn't do anything about the wings, of course. They emerged from a slit in the back of the jacket, but the angel had made some attempt to conceal their bulk under a light raincoat. He was a sad and comical figure, and his glow was almost gone.

On an instinct I grabbed my own coat and followed him when he left, hurrying to catch up with him, only to hang back. I can't say if he saw me or not.

It was another cold winter's day. Scattered flakes of snow spiralled out of a blue sky, winking out of existence moments after they landed. I wondered if the angel saw them and thought of home?

The angel could only have seen the town that one time, on the day of his arrival, but he seemed to know where he was heading – up along the main road, turning left where the shops began. From thirty feet behind I saw him enter the newsagents.

By the time I hurried through the door, the shop was already silent. Customers stood frozen, watching the angel move along the rows of packaged goods. He drifted past the newspapers and the magazines without a glance, and selected items from the shelves: bread, washcloths, a jar of mustard. It seemed to me that every choice was random. He needed none of it, recognised none of it. His aim was to fit in, nothing more. When he placed the items wordlessly on the counter he paid in government vouchers.

A gaggle of people followed him out of the shop. Someone must have slipped next door to spread the word, because a miniature crowd was gathering. Faces pressed against shop windows; curious children were thrust back by nervous parents; the angel seemed oblivious. He had turned to head back home, presenting his partially covered wings to the mob.

A shout! A shove! A sudden outcry of fear and rage!

I spun, trying to see who had yelled, just in time to see a rock fly from the crowd and strike the angel in the shoulder. He stumbled and fell, and I saw the red faced stranger from the park, arm raised in anger, clutching a second stone in his hand.

There was an instant of confusion. People scattered. The red faced man lunged towards the angel and ripped the raincoat from his back. There were feathers in the air, and blood on the ground. The man raised his rock again, but I put myself in the way and he hesitated.

Then I was away, with the angel in my arms.

He was as light as a feather, weighing barely more than his clothes. When I reached the stairs he wrapped one wing around my shoulders for support, and limped beside me.

Back in the quiet safety of his flat I peeled the clothing from his body and used a wet flannel to dab the blood away. His pale skin was already bruising where blows had struck him. His flesh was as translucent as alabaster and, naked, it glowed from within.

The angel knelt on the bare floorboards and looked up at me. His eyes were like windows into somewhere else. Looking into them I seemed to see a sky as endless as the sea; a palace of cloud castles and sunbeams, where throngs of angels swarmed in unison like starlings. I understood that this was where the angels belonged, and I yearned for it as if it had been my own home.

I looked away.

Later I heard a noise from his flat I couldn't identify. I pressed my head against the thin plaster wall, hoping to hear the brush of wings or the murmur of song, but there was only silence.

In the morning the angel was gone.

The door to his flat stood open, and I trembled to see drops of blood smeared on the stone of the landing. There was nothing in the kitchen, the bedroom, or the hall. There was no sign of the coat, the hat, the regulation suitcase. He had even taken the bread and the mustard – everything he might need to vanish amongst humans.

I hesitated at the bedroom door, knowing what I would find. Inside it was like a slaughterhouse. The bare boards were stained red, the walls too. Blood and feathers were strewn about, and a kitchen knife lay discarded amongst the grey-white plumage.

The angel had cut off his wings.

B

… is for **Bestiary**

Misidentification

Hey Hazel! How have you been keeping? Sorry that it's been a while since I wrote, been busy, same old same old. Ha ha!

Well, almost. The strangest thing has been happening to me, you'll never believe it.

It started while I was taking a walk in the woods. You know that I've been trying to lose a bit of weight, and a Saturday afternoon trek down into the valley seemed like a good idea. It was cold, frosty, quite pretty really.

I'd been out about an hour, and had just got down to where the stream is, when I saw something weird on the path. A lizard! In the woods! It was about a foot long, with dramatic black and orange markings all over its body. It had a club-shaped sort of tail, with three ridges on top, and a wide flat head.

Well, of course I knew it wasn't supposed to be there. There are no lizards like that round here! My first thought was that it was someone's escaped pet, but then what was it doing all the way out in the woods? So that meant someone had dumped it, poor thing!

And it didn't look at all well. It was sort of on its side, and sluggish. Its eyes were milky white, and I thought it might have been blind. It certainly didn't seem to notice that I was there.

I felt really angry. I'm not a great lizard fan, but how could anyone just leave a pet out to die like that? I took it home of course, wrapped up in my coat. I thought it would be slimy, but its skin was rough, like textured wallpaper. And it was cold, really cold. I remember hoping that my body heat might warm it up a little.

Back home I put it in a box and tried looking online to see if I could work out what it was. It was easy to tell that it wasn't a local animal, but after that I struggled. You wouldn't believe how many different lizards there are! I found a number of things that looked a bit like it, but I couldn't find a match. I did find a reptile shop that wasn't far away, but that wouldn't help the poor thing at 6pm on a Saturday night.

Turns out lizards eat all sorts of awful things that I didn't have around the house, like locusts, and crickets, and worms. But I did find one site that told me you could feed a lizard prawns, and I had some of them in the fridge, so that was okay. I warmed some up in the microwave, (did you know that lizards eat their food hot?), and waved them under his nose. (I'd decided on 'he' based on nothing really, sorry if that's sexist.) That got his attention!

The milky eyes turned out to be eyelids, I guess, because suddenly there was a pair of yellow eyes staring at the prawn in my fingers. They practically glowed with hunger. The lizard darted forward and I dropped the prawn in surprise.

That was when I knew for sure that I wasn't going to find this lizard on any reptile site!

Fire! It breathed fire! Honest to God, Hazel. It breathed a gout of fire straight on that prawn, and then snapped it up.

I had a dragon! Can you imagine what I was feeling? You know me, I don't do fantasy, but I couldn't argue with what I'd seen.

It didn't look like any dragon I'd ever heard of, but what do I know. Maybe this is what baby dragons look like. Maybe I had to wait till it grew wings or something? I tried to imagine how it had gotten in the woods. The phantom pet-abandoning owner didn't make any sense now. Had it hatched from an egg? Was there a mummy dragon out there somewhere? Was there some sort of law about these things? One thing seemed clear to me, I wasn't going to take it to the pet shop. I mean, it could have been worth a fortune!

I put it in a shoe box with some paper towels and a little dish of water, and put the whole thing in the bathroom; because of the fire-breathing. Just as well! Sometime in the night the whole thing must have gone up. All the bath contained in the morning was soot, a dragon, and a bowl.

I moved it to a plastic box, but that got melted a few days later, by which point I'd found an old fish tank for it to live in. I'd visited the pet shop too, but it didn't want any of the weird foods I'd been sold, just prawns. It loved prawns. As many as I was willing to give it, and it was visibly growing by eating them, which made me worried — but I couldn't let it starve, could I?

I was still trying to work out what to do with the thing. If it would just grow wings, or get photogenic, or something, then maybe I could make some money out of it. Or maybe I should be giving it over to science? I don't mind telling you that I was getting pretty worried about having it around.

When I woke up to find that it had started to melt the glass, I panicked. I had to get it out of the house! I put it in the car, intending to take it to the pet shop, but then I started to wonder what they would do with it. Would they look after it? Would they sell it to someone for experiments? So instead I drove back to the woods and put it where I had found it, with a few prawns and a little shelter. I felt bad about putting it back into the cold, but I was sure it would be okay. I mean, it could breathe fire!

That night, (this was Monday), I woke up to the smell of smoke. I rushed back into the living room and saw the lizard, sitting in the middle of a circle of smouldering carpet! I'd left it three miles away and it was back!

When I tried to pick it up it was cold! As cold as ice, but my clothing started to char in moments! What could I do? I managed to get it in a metal box, and threw the box in the car. Then I drove, still half dressed, as far as I could and dumped the box under a hedgerow. I know, I know; but honestly I'd stopped worrying about the lizard, it could take care of itself.

By the time I got home the lizard was already there, sitting in the hallway five feet from the hole it had melted in the front door.

I went back on the 'net, with one eye on the lizard, which I'd left in a pile of frozen prawns dragged out of the freezer.

Turns out there is a thing called a Salamander. Not the newt thing you find in lakes, but a mythical beast that starts fires. Sound familiar? A Salamander is always cold, but things around it catch fire. It can even live in flames! The Greeks had some funny legends about it, but nothing about it following someone around, or teleporting cross-country, or whatever it did.

I knew that was it. I had to pass it on to someone else. First thing in the morning was what I told myself. I put it in the freezer – with the door open of course – and went to bed.

I woke up in the middle of the night to roaring flames. It was awful. I lost everything. I nearly didn't get out. I had to crawl through the window half naked, and believe me I didn't stop to look for that bloody lizard! I lost the whole house. It was burnt to the ground.

Which brings me to the main reason I was getting in touch. I don't suppose you still have that spare room available do you? The one in the barn?

Don't worry about the Salamander. I'm sure it's gone now.

Pretty sure, anyway.

Hoping to hear back from you soon, Michael

C

... is for **Clouds**

Mr Martello and the Cloud Castle

Mr Martello paused on his way to work to stare at a cloud castle which had come to rest above the steeply peaked rooftops of the University.

Although most of the people hurrying through the streets didn't notice, it was a particularly fine example of the breed; with soaring spires of cumulus rising above a central keep of bright white cloud. Blue-grey shadows marked an arching frontage, speckled with sunlit cornices and streaming banners of vapour. Underneath its rolling basements seagulls hung on the air, pointing their faces into the gale.

Mr Martello happened to be something of an expert on cloud formations. He saw at once that the top heavy towers of the cloud castle had been inspired by the baroque fantasies of Neuschwanstein, which suggested that its builder was possessed of a certain degree of culture. Although a visit would undoubtedly make him late for work, Mr Martello felt that this would be a price worth paying.

Of course the castle hung at least a thousand feet above the city, but this was no obstacle to Mr Martello, who always carried an oversized golf umbrella for just such occasions. He angled it in the direction of the castle, and was instantly plucked up by the wind. He shot up over the heads of a pair of pinstriped gentlemen, clutching their bowler hats to their heads, with barely time for an "Excuse me"; and in moments was up over the rooftops.

Soon Mr Martello found himself settling into the middle

of a fluffy white courtyard, surrounded by tenuous cirrus topiaries. Gingerly he tested the spongy surface to make sure that it would hold his weight, then furled his umbrella. There was a circular hole in the middle of the cloudy floor through which the distant spires of the University were just visible. Mr Martello leant a little way over to take in the view, then stowed his umbrella neatly under his left arm and headed inside.

The hallways of the cloud castle were vast and soaring, lit by clerestories of sunlight and cages of chained lightning. Cloud portraits adorned the walls, their wispy faces looming over the top of Mr Martello's head as he ventured deeper.

There were many chambers in as many shades of grey; pewter, slate, lead, military, and storm. Mr Martello noted them with professional interest in a small buckram notebook, but he was really in search of the castle's owners, or at the very least a servant.

The next chamber Mr Martello entered formed the soaring base of one of the castle's towers. It was as circular as the eye of a tornado, with restless spiral walls that met far above his head. He attempted to count that various twisting strands, but it was a fruitless endeavour, as they would not stay still long enough to be counted.

When he lowered his eyes again he found that he had been joined by an inhabitant of the castle. It resembled nothing so much as a miniature tornado, poorly formed, and he quickly identified it as a menial of some sort.

"My name is Mr Martello," he said — his first words since arriving at the castle. "Please convey my respects to your Master or Mistress."

The tornado inclined its upper rim in his direction, and then moved towards one of the chambers' many exits before pausing to wait for him; which Mr Martello took to be an invitation to follow.

The Countess Wolke, when Mr Martello was ushered into

her presence, was built to the same scale as her castle. Which is to say that she towered above him. Two columns of cumulonimbus were perched on the top of her stately head, somewhat in the shape of an elongated heart, which increased her height still further. Under the headpiece she wore a veil of slate-grey raindrops, which served to accentuate the paleness of her face.

The Countess acknowledged Mr Martello's arrival with an imperious wave of one cloud-white hand, which also served as an invitation to come closer to her throne.

Mr Martello delivered a neat little bow, removing his bowler hat, and made his introductions. After a few polite observations on the peculiarities of the castle's construction, and a cordial compliment on the Countess's attention to detail, he ventured a question.

"I wonder if you might indulge my curiosity," he began. "I am something of a scholar in matters of Nephology (which is the study of clouds), and so I am aware that it is very unusual to see a cloud dwelling of such quality in so prosaic a town as ours. Was there a particular reason you chose this course?"

"The Count and I," the Countess indicated her anaemic looking husband with a vaporous gesture, "have been robbed!"

The Count, a far less imposing figure than the Countess, drifted hurriedly forward, descending the stratus steps in a swirl of damp precipitation.

"What the Countess means … ahem … is that our prize collection has gone missing."

The Count pointed out a series of empty plinths and alcoves around the chamber in which their collection had until recently been displayed. A few remaining examples made the nature of the missing collection clear — cloud shapes of the most classic kind. Dragons, sailing ships, mountain ranges, and woolly sheep. The type of things that any young schoolboy, or summer couple, might look up into the sky and imagine.

"I don't suppose," the Count said self-effacingly, that you might have any idea ..."

The trouble was that Mr Martello rather did. Being something of an expert on the subject, he knew (as apparently the Count and Countess did not) that the shapes of clouds are summoned mostly by the eye of the beholder. Should a group of schoolboys, say, gather on a hillside near where the castle had been passing and stare at the sky expectantly, the Countesses' prize collection would have come running to appear.

It so happened that Mr Martello had been leading just such a trip into the hills the previous day, a fact that he rather thought it politic not to mention to the Countess. Instead he launched into an erudite sort of denial that would have amazed the company at the University dramatic society, who had always regarded Mr Martello as the least plausible of actors.

Sadly the Countess Wolke had seen more than her share of professional thespians in the upper atmosphere, and saw through Mr Martello's protestations at once. The Count had barely time to start mumbling his regrets before she interrupted with a thunderous: "Thief!"

"Benji!" she screeched, "Benji! This man is the thief!"

Mr Martello thought that it would be tactful to withdraw at this point. He placed his bowler hat neatly back on his head and made his farewells, retreating rapidly back into the vestibule as he did so, before turning to hurry back the way he had come. Behind him he could hear the shrill voice of the Count ordering his Altostratus guards to give chase.

Fortunately Mr Martello had made extensive notes on the chambers he had passed on his way in. Unfortunately he didn't really have time to look at them while running. Instead he beat a hasty retreat through the nearest exit, hoping that he might find himself on a balcony, in a courtyard, or at the entrance to a fog garden.

Instead he found his way blocked by a mass of ice crystals, as fine as rain drops, which were circulating up and down at speed in a crevasse between thunderheads. He made to turn back, but the corridor was full of militant whirlwinds making their approach.

"Allez Oop!" said Mr Martello, which was the only French he knew, and opened his umbrella into the curtain of ice.

Mr Martello held a faint hope that the circular wind might carry him gently back to the University — where he was now quite overdue for a lecture — but instead it plucked him straight up to the top of one of the castle's soaring Bavarian spires.

A loose spiral of fluffy cumulus led down the outside of the tower, each step floating a few feet below the previous one, but Mr Martello didn't try to run down them, because he had noticed something slightly alarming — the castle was starting to change shape.

Mr Martello was familiar with the fact that a cloud shape studied overlong will inevitably transform into something else. No amount of wishful thinking can prevent a cloud lion from turning into a lamb, or a ship into a hummingbird, if once you start to stare at it. So it was with the castle. Now that the Count and Countess were concentrating on searching the cloud for him, rather than keeping their minds on their collection, it was starting to change.

At any other time Mr Martello would have been fascinated to observe the process from close up, and indeed he made a few quick observations to commit to his notebook later, but the surface under his feet was already starting to lose its cohesion. Whatever the cloud castle had decided to change into evidently did not have towers.

Mr Martello turned to his umbrella once again, leaping off

the toppling tower towards the castle's more extensive lower levels. He came to rest amongst the rapidly dissolving cumulus of the Countess' ballroom, but the white expanse of the floor no longer bore his weight. Instead it swallowed his feet right up to the knees, rather – Mr Martello thought – like a bath full of taffy. With dogged determination he pushed himself toward what appeared to be a more substantial layer of blue-grey stratus, but he had not yet reached it when the wispy cloud behind him tore apart and the Countess came rushing through, one of the captive lightning bolts crackling in her hand.

"Madam!" Mr Martello exclaimed, hoping to check her advance, but the Countess bore on, dragging half the castle's wind and rain behind her!

"Thief!"

Mr Martello dearly wished to correct the Countess' misunderstanding, but he'd read enough about cloud culture to conclude that discretion might be the better part of valour. A letter, he concluded, might always be dispatched at a later date with a better explanation.

Accordingly Mr Martello deployed his trusty umbrella one last time, grasping it firmly in his right hand while using his left to steady the bowler hat against his head. In this manner he leapt neatly off the edge of the cloud and away.

A little while later, having got his feet back on solid ground, Mr Martello tried to spot the cloud castle again, but though he could see many splendid clouds soaring overhead, none were recognisable. Moreover, when he took the time to look around at ground level, he was a little dismayed to see that he had been carried well beyond the edge of town, and had been deposited amongst the very same hills he'd hiked though the day before. His class would now most certainly be canceled rather than simply run late.

'Still,' he reflected, patting his meteorological notebook happily, it had been a particularly fine cloud castle!

D

… is for **Dendrology** (the study of trees)

The Cherry Tree

The Doctor's diagnosis of fatal arborification was not in any way welcome, as I am sure you can imagine, but it was at least delivered in time for me to set my affairs in order.

When the first woody patches started to appear on my arms, I had tried to ignore them. They were silver grey. At first they flaked away readily when touched, but soon they bedded in, and little threads extended out beneath my skin. When I ran my fingers over them I could feel their thickness. I knew what it was, of course, but it was not until the first roots began to poke their way between my toes that I forced myself to seek the obvious medical opinion.

Luckily I was a man of few friends and no family. Putting my social and legal affairs in order was a simple matter. In other people, no doubt, it would have been an occasion for wailing, sorrow, and depression, but I have always found it easier to accept fate than struggle against it. The hardest part was finding a new home for my cat, Maribel. I knew that she would not understand when I became less able to care for her.

A more difficult problem was deciding what my own fate should be. Lacking a family to look after me, I determined that I should be planted in the wild, where nature could take care of me in her own traditional manner, but this required some idea of what sort of tree I was turning into. It wouldn't do to secure a spot amongst the Christmas trees and then discover that I was becoming a coconut palm. By the time I put out recognisable leaves I'd already be rooted.

I returned to the Doctor. There exist organisations dedicated to the care of arboritis sufferers, experts in matters dendritic. With my Doctor's encouragement I made arrangements with the National Arboreal Society. For a modest fee their botanists would conduct a bark and xylem identification, and recommend a suitable habitat for my final resting place. By the time I met with Mrs Rowlands the early emergence of buds at my hairline made her identification easy, and I was pleased to learn that I was soon to become a *Prunus Cerasifera* – a Cherry Plum.

The Cherry Plum is an ornamental tree, with bright pink blossoms and a spreading cloud of branches. It reminded me of a tree I had seen before, at the corner of the town park in Marchester, where I first met her. I'd never sat under that tree myself, but I'd stared at it often.

When I visited the park I saw that the tree I remembered was no longer there. It had died many years before and the spot had been left vacant. I made enquiries and discovered that it would be possible to be planted there, where others might see me.

Soon I was ensconced in the park, at first in a wheelchair, then later, as my roots became established, standing comfortably a little way off from the path, where I could still exchange complacencies with passing walkers and yet not scare the children. Towards the end, the Arboreal Society were able to have a decorative bench erected beside my trunk, and it pleased me to think that, come the spring, young couples might stop to rest under my display of blossoms – as she and I had never sat.

Should you visit the park, and find yourself upon the bench that bears my name, perhaps you too will stay a while to admire my blossoms, and place a hand upon my trunk for old times sake.

E

... is for **Enigma**

The Face under my bed

There is a face under my bed.

I saw it for the first time late on a Saturday night, when I'd had too much to drink and was none too sober. I heard a rustling under the bed and suspected mice. I hung my head over the edge, like a drunken monkey, and fished around for a view of it, using my phone like a searchlight.

When I saw those huge white eyes staring back at me I dropped the phone and nearly dropped myself!

After that my bed became an island in a sea of danger. I cowered in the middle, too scared to put a foot over the side in case something grabbed it. I was so certain that the face was coming for me that I imagined claws groping their way blindly up the covers towards me and held onto them desperately.

Turns out the face has no hands, and I guess the poor guy was as scared as I was, because he was right below me – in the centre of the under-bed – the whole time.

I know this because we started talking – well what else was I going to do? At first all I could hear were whispers, creepy as fuck, like something right out of a horror movie. I put my fingers in my ears, but the whispering didn't stop. So I shouted incoherently back, swearing and cursing, until I realised that the face wasn't really whispering, it was just muffled by two foot of mattress. Once we'd exchanged a few intelligible words – names, insults, begging – it started to tell me about itself.

The face, it seems, has quite a lot of insecurities, but a philosophical bent on life that's quite appropriate for the middle of the night. It is almost companionable, in the way that the guy on the next barstool might be — up for talking all night through.

Which is a good thing.

Because no way in hell am I getting out of this bed!

F

… is for **Feline**

Feline Solutions to Alien Problems

With one prodigious bound Maribel leapt from the windowsill outside the bedroom, right across the yawning gap to the sloping roof of the garden shed. From there it was an easy run along the top of the fence to the bottom of the garden, where she could hop down into the narrow lane that ran between her garden and the next.

Another cat lay sprawled along the top of the wall beyond the fence, enjoying the warmth of the early morning sunlight that slanted across the stones; but Maribel paid no attention to him. It was only Ginger, the fat tabby from next door. Ginger, for his part, hardly managed to open one lazy eye before Maribel had jumped over him, with a flash of her delicate paws, and was off down the lane.

At the end of the lane there was a hedge, which ran up the hill towards the woods that overlooked the village. Maribel crouched under the lowest branches, paws in, head down, and whiskers forward. Only the tip of her tail twitched, and she wasn't even aware of that.

The hedge provided the only route to the woods, other than the open fields where Maribel had no intention of going, but it was the territory of Luna, the black and white queen who was also Maribel's nemesis. Maribel was quick, sleek, and elegant — the finest looking tortoiseshell in the village, if she said so herself; but she was also small where Luna was big. When Luna hunted along the hedge, Maribel would slip back home with her tail down.

Luckily there was no sign of Luna that day, and soon

Maribel had crossed the length of the hedge, and was out on the hilltop that none of the cats claimed as their own.

Here the grass grew long and wild, filled with tiny things that ran, and hid, and tasted fascinating. Little birds hopped from stem to stem, close enough to the ground to be caught in a single leap, and even tinier mice scampered through the tangled roots, perfect for games of pounce and play. Sometimes Maribel spent hours here, hunting, or sunning herself in the grass; returning home with a dead mouse as a gift for her human.

But the real attraction was the wood. Maribel loved to stare at it, but had never been inside. It smelt different to the fields. It smelt of loam, and leaves, and foxes, and badgers. She was torn between the desire to explore and the fear of the unknown. She would turn her back on the trees, groom herself, and tell herself that she wasn't really that interested anyway.

Today there was a new smell in the air, something that Maribel didn't recognise. When she cocked her ears forward and listened, she could hear a distant humming noise that came from somewhere amongst the trees. She didn't like it, but it fascinated her anyway.

Cautiously Maribel slunk between the trees on her belly, making no more than the slightest of rustles. The wood was thick with soft loam, and dead leaves, and dapples of sunlight that formed stepping stones on the way to the noise.

In the middle of the woods there was a pool. Although Maribel didn't know it, the wood had once been the site of a quarry. Now the flooded quarry pit formed a circular pond with a steep rocky bank sloping down to it on one side. Oak trees crowded the top of this cliff, their branches overhanging the water.

Near to the edge of the water three curious creatures were standing. They were pale grey, egg-shaped, no larger than kittens – balanced upright on their broad ends. From where she crouched amongst the fallen branches, Maribel could see that their lower halves were actually tight-packed clusters of tentacles, like fingers pressed together. Maribel had never seen an octopus, of course. If she had, she might have thought that these creatures looked a little like them.

The three creatures were looking up at one of the trees, where the source of the humming was lodged. It was something like a large flat food dish, the same grey as the creatures, with flickering lights along the edge. It was balanced at an angle, stuck between two branches, as if it had fallen off a higher bit of the tree and gotten stuck.

Maribel had never seen anything like these creatures. In her curiosity she forgot all about being sneaky. She went over to them with her tail held high and kinked at the top. They didn't seem to notice her at first, so she batted one with an exploratory paw. To her surprise it was hard and smooth, like the pottery owl her human kept on the shelf.

The creatures turned in surprise, their stubby legs clicking on the ground. They had large blue eyes, and appeared to regard her with amazement. Maribel wasn't sure whether they were dangerous, edible, or friendly, so she sat back with her tail wrapped neatly around her paws and waited to see what they did.

The creatures glanced at each other and exchanged rapid words while Maribel listened with perked ears. After a few moments they appeared to come to some sort of decision, because one of them hopped forward and began to speak to Maribel, gesticulating with its legs all the while – so that sometimes it was standing on five legs, sometimes three, and, once, balancing on two.

Maribel had no idea what the creature was saying, of course. She understood only cat, and a few words of owner that she rarely condescended to pay attention to. But she followed the movement of the creature's feet with fascination, jerking her head back and forth to keep up with the motion.

The creature kept pointing up at the humming thing in the tree. They were asking her for help, of course, but helping is not something cats understand. Still, the humming thing in the tree looked quite fascinating, and Maribel decided to go up and have a look at it.

She sized up the tree, then leapt her way up a series of branches, until she was balanced cautiously on a branch a couple of feet away from the thing stuck in the tree. From close up it looked rather like two giant saucers pressed together face to face, with lights winking in the channel between the two rims. It reminded her of a toy that her owner had once bought her, which had tasty treats inside, only this one was a lot bigger and so might have bigger treats!

She stuck her paw experimentally into the gap in the rim and scrabbled around in the hope that something might fall out. The disk shifted alarmingly back and forth – it was only lightly wedged between two smaller branches. When no food came out, Maribel rubbed her face against its sharp edge to mark it with her scent, and knocked it from its perch.

Maribel sprang back in alarm, squeezing herself into a fork in the branch, and watched as the disk plummeted to the ground below. It landed on its edge, wobbling. For a moment looked as if it might fall flat on the ground – and this appeared to please the tiny creatures, who twittered in happiness far below; but instead of falling it rolled along the ground, straight off the edge of the cliff.

By the time Maribel joined the creatures at the edge of the cliff, only a faint patch of bubbles marked the place where the humming object had vanished into the water.

The creatures jumped up and down in agitation, clacking their little feet together and rolling their eyes. One of them kept gesturing towards the water with jerky motions of one of its feet – so Maribel gave it a little paw-tap and knocked it off the edge.

Down the creature went with a high pitched wail, until it landed in the water with a splash. What fun!

One of the two remaining creatures gave such a sharp cry that Maribel arched her back and jumped away in surprise. Ignoring her, it started to scramble down the steep slope towards the water, although its stiff little legs were no good for climbing.

The remaining creature shook its limbs at Maribel and babbled at her as if outraged. It reminded her of the times that her owner got angry and shook his finger at her. She didn't like it when he did that. Every time he did, she made sure to trip him up later, or to wait behind the bedroom door and bite him on the ankle when he went past. This creature irritated her even more, because its finger was right in her nose. She hissed, and arched her back more, but it didn't back off — so as soon as it turned away to see what its friends were doing she pounced on it, knocked it down, and bit it where its shell joined its legs.

It struggled in her jaws for a moment, mewling pitifully, but she was already trotting away with it, feeling proud of herself. Still carrying the creature she snaked through the long grass and down under the hedge back to the lane, passed lightly past the sleeping Ginger, and sprung back to the fence beside the garden. Finally she slipped through the open window back into the bedroom.

It was still early in the morning, and Maribel's owner was sleeping in his bed — so she deposited the mostly dead creature on his pillow, and then sat back to await his praise for a job well done.

G

… is for **Gastric**

Sickness

I retch, groan, attempt to vomit, but my insides are stopped up with pain; nothing but white spit makes it out. Some creature, writhing in my gut, contains it all.

I can feel it, heavy and malignant, weighing down my stomach like a stone. When it twists; tunnels deep through my intestines; ties knots; bites with sharp fangs — I also writhe, groan, and gnash my teeth in fruitless frustration. I want to force it out, but it will not go.

When I try to sleep, side-down under the press of covers, it stretches out, pushing my organs against my skin, then contracts itself till my guts bloat around it. I am wracked by pain, but it stirs in contentment. It has grown huge by gorging itself on all evils I've bottled up inside of me.

It has devoured my fears, my petty hatreds, my gross anxieties. It has dined on my personal panics; fattened itself on neuroses; suckled sustenance from my grudges. When I swallow my pride it snaps it up, digests it in the convolutions of my duodenum, and spits it back in the form of acid bile.

I hear its rumbles and its gurgles, its vitriol and its spite. It spews the leftovers of my own words back at me. It plagues me with regurgitated worries and turgid terrors. It latches onto the whirling confusion of my mind and injects venom from its fangs.

I clamp my hands over my ears, but it forces its way up the length of my oesophagus to rasp against my eardrums from the inside, so that I cannot avoid it. It has grown so fat that my swollen body can no longer contain its bile.

Only now does it allow me to vomit, pushing its way out through my pores, my throat, my tear ducts — shedding me like an old skin. When I fall slack it drops into the toilet bowl; consumes its own afterbirth; grows animate; hurls its way into the world to propagate.

Only now, for a little while, can I sleep.

H

… is for **Heat**

My Powerstation Wife

When the Mayor first suggested using my wife as power station for the town, it seemed like a sensible idea.

My wife has always been hot. Not beautiful you understand – though she is that too – but high temperature. Not in the sense that she is on fire, but immensely warm regardless of the circumstances. When I turned the heating up she turned it down. When winter came she kept the window open. When the freezing wind came down out of the mountains and buried the town under snow, she headed out in a t-shirt. I had never needed a hot water bottle to heat up my bed.

I wasn't the only person to notice her heat. It was a running joke around the town, but a good natured one. Her heart had always been as warm as her body, and just as sustaining. When the idea of using some of that warmth to supply the town came up she was the first to approve of it. "I want to help," was what she always said.

Apparently the Mayor came up with the idea because of some new funding initiative. Renewable energy would bring attractive tax breaks, and my wife was always into saving the planet.

When the Mayor first broached the idea, during the coffee that followed a pleasant dinner party, it sounded innocuous enough. Warm air would be extracted from the room where my wife worked and used to heat the school next door. She positively glowed at the idea. I could feel the warmth across the table.

Only the plan didn't really work.

Oh the air warmed up all right. The problem was that it didn't warm up enough. According to the power station technicians, with their white coats and maroon clipboards, my wife never got cold, but she never got hot enough either. There was a loss of heat at every step of the process. After five different inefficiencies – wife to air, air to hot water, hot water to radiator, and so forth – half the useful heat was lost.

They installed fans in the office first, then huge compressors that whined and roared like asthmatic lions. I tried to follow their explanations as to why, but I lost them when they began to talk about *thermobaric efficiency*. They sealed the edges of the windows and the door with thick bands of foam and rubber. When you opened the door at the end of the day it was like stepping into the wrong end of a wind tunnel.

When the school was finally declared warm enough we celebrated, but they wanted more. They talked about heat for the hospital; for the nursery; for the Mayor's house. More men came – grey suited experts from the Ministry of Power. They made the air cold, then wet, then wet and cold. They seemed pleased with the results. They were heating half the town by then, but the Mayor had plans. He wanted hot water, steam generators, re-election.

When they moved her to the first of the liquid facilities I begged her to stop. She would come home wrinkled and aching, unused to the pull of gravity after so long suspended in water, and collapse on the bed, good for nothing. I'd been pleased when I'd seen her in the first custom wetsuit – I knew how much she loved swimming – but the hours had relentlessly increased until she was more marine battery than woman. I held her in my arms – still warm of course, even after everything – and told her that enough was enough.

"I just want to do my part," she whispered. "The people

need me."

"I need you!"

In the end even a heart as generous as hers had limits. She decided to stop, only it turned out not to be quite that easy. The Ministry people presented me with documents; with contracts that my wife didn't remember signing; with a hundred page regional sustainability report that made it clear that the town was now legally in control of my wife's heat.

I went to war with the government. I hired a big-shot lawyer from the capitol, who drove down in a reassuringly expensive car to contest the Ministry bureaucrats. He spent long hours on the intercom to my wife — they kept her entirely underwater by that point — spending the generous money that they'd given her early on, before being a power station had become a civic duty. We went to court, we held appeals.

We lost.

I've heard that they've switched from water to some sort of oil now, for better efficiency. There was a program about it on the town TV station. I wouldn't know first hand, they don't let me see her in person any more.

But I can still feel her — when I press my face against the hot water pipes. Even after all this, she is still warm.

I

… is for **Invisible**

Arthur

It's been a while, James thought, as he turned his car into his father's driveway; years actually, when he thought about it. Work, then bankruptcy, and then the divorce – of course – had kept him away. Now, looking at the familiar whitewashed walls of the house, he felt a vague prickling of annoyance – surely his father must be lonely, living alone in a house intended for a family. Well, he was here to take care of that now.

His father seemed well enough when he met him at the door – took his suitcase with good grace; made the expected joke about how he knew the way – but the house seemed cold to James, too big for one old man to rattle around in.

When he settled down in the living room he put both hands on his knees, leant forward in what he hoped was a sympathetic manner, and broached the subject.

"So, Dad, how are you doing?"

"Oh, can't complain lad."

"You aren't … lonely?" James had placed some brochures for the Cherry Tree Residential Home in his bag before setting out. All he had to do now was get him to agree to a move, and then he could set about selling the house. It was all for the best.

"Lonely? Nawwww. I've got Arthur to keep me company."

"Arthur?" James was nonplussed. He racked his memory

for an Arthur. Had he been mentioned in one of his father's infrequent letters? Was he a carer? a neighbour? an old friend? God forbid his dad had turned gay and found a partner!

"The dog, James," the old man smiled, "Arthur's the dog."

James felt a sense of relief, and he realised that he'd seen a lead hanging by the front door and an overstuffed cushion on the floor in the spare room. Still, there was no reason he should have guessed, his father had never owned a dog before.

"You've got a dog then Dad?"

His father gave him a strange look. "Aye, that's him on the sofa."

James stared at the sofa — there was nothing there.

"Funny story," his father continued, apparently oblivious, "never really wanted a dog, but there was this terrible storm a few months back and I heard this scratching at the door. When I went to answer it, there was a dog, all soaking wet. Well, what was I to do?"

James wasn't listening. Had his father gone mad? Could he just be blind, and not know that the dog was somewhere else? No, he'd taken his case at the door … he wasn't blind. Had to be crazy then, and that was going to mean something a lot more hardcore than Cherry Tree Residential Home, something psychiatric, something expensive!

"And then," his father was saying, "I got the idea to call him Arthur. Odd name for a dog you might think, but I think it suits him." And then to the empty sofa opposite, "Who's a good boy then Arthur? Eh boy?"

"There's nothing there Dad!"

"'Course there is. Losing your sight are you son? Why don't you go over there and say hello. He won't bite."

James found himself getting out of his seat, more to stall

for time than anything else. He stared down at the empty sofa, taking in the dimpled cushions and the folded dog blanket. He actually had a dog blanket!

"Give him a pet."

James had no idea how to treat a mad person. He remembered something about humouring them, and so he put out a hand and stroked the empty air, hoping it would make the old man happy.

And heard a growl.

"Arthur!" His father shook a finger at the sofa, but James was already backing away, reversing until the back of his legs struck the edge of his chair, where he sat down with a thump.

"He's usually such a good dog, sorry about that."

James' mind whirled. Infectious hallucinations? An actual invisible dog? Some stray noise that he'd misheard? James told himself that it must be the last one. He'd wanted to humour his father, and got carried away. It was almost funny when you thought about it. And he was justified in having a little wobble, after all, he hadn't planned for this!

Once he'd taken a sip of his tea the whole thing seemed a lot simpler. His father's delusion was harmless, when you thought about it. Maybe Cherry Tree was still on the cards after all, he just had to make a really convincing case, or … what if he had him committed? Wouldn't that be free?

His father stood up with an arthritic groan. "Well I better get the dinner on, I'm sure you must be hungry."

James nodded absently, relieved to be free of the problem of the invisible dog for a little while. He began to think about what to do in the morning, who to phone, what he would do with the house, when he heard his father call through from the kitchen.

"James! Could you give us a hand and take Arthur out for his walk? Just take him to the corner and back, lead's by the door."

James froze in his chair. What was he to do? If he objected it might start a fight, and he needed to keep his dad onside until he could call in a professional and get him dealt with. Put that way, there was only one option: keep humouring him.

He went to the door and took down the dog lead, then stared dumbly at it. Should he take it with him? Of course he should. He made to head out, but then his father was in the hallway, fussing.

"You've not done it up right lad," he said, pointing at the dangling lead. "See, you clip it on here." He reached down and attached the catch at the end of the lead to nothing. "There you are. Now off you go."

A moment later James was standing on the doorstep, feeling the bite of the night air through his thin coat. Could he sit in his car for ten minutes and then go back? But no, it would be just like the old man to see him out of the window. Instead he turned up his collar and headed down the drive towards the street.

He hadn't made it two steps before something else took over.

With an almighty tug the lead snatched at him, exactly as if some enormous dog was attached to the other end. He'd looped the handle of the lead around his wrist, was dragged down the drive by it. He dug his fingers under the leather strap, trying desperately to lever it free, but suddenly he was slammed face first into the privet hedge.

James tried to yell for help, but his mouth was full of leaves. Branches scraped at his face, sharp twigs stabbed into his cheeks. It was all he could do to clamp his left hand over his face before he lost an eye.

He came out the other side of the hedge on his belly. The lead dragged him on, arm outstretched, through gutters, mud, overflowing rubbish sacks. He screamed, but the suburban streets were empty, and there was nothing at the end of the lead.

When he tried to get his feet wedged against the edge of the kerb the invisible dog growled at him, a deep throaty menace that told him to stay still and suffer, but James was frantic. He grabbed at a passing lamppost with his free hand, swinging himself around till the post was wedged against his stomach. He folded himself in half, clinging to the post by the pressure of his knees and tore the lead from his wrist.

The lead whipped away, the end describing a tight circle in the air, still attached to a collar which was in turn attached to nothing, and, just for a moment, passed into shadow. In that moment James finally saw the invisible dog.

Jumbled impressions: eyes as big as saucers; teeth like kitchen knives; three mouths or more, bursting out from inside each other; tails of bone and naked sinew, all revealed for an eye-blink by the darkness.

James ran and didn't stop running.

Later, James' father opened the front door to the sound of insistent scratching.

"Hey there boy!" He rubbed the back of Arthur's neck cheerfully, detaching the lead and peering out into the yellow-tinged gloom.

"No sign of that son of mine? No, there wouldn't be. Look at these boy, see what I found upstairs." He waved a sheaf of pastel coloured leaflets in Arthur's direction. "Wanted to pack me off to an old folks home, he did! Well, good riddance to him. I don't need him - I've got you!"

He chuckled cheerfully and shut the door.

"Now come on boy, it's dinner time."

J

… is for **Jinn** (a spirit of the air)

Milk for the Wind

The wind wakes me.

It is caterwauling outside the window, howling and scratching at the glass. Now it scrabbles back and forth over the rooftop. Now it leaps from tree to tree, testing each protesting branch to see if it will break. Now it roars and moans in frustration.

There is something pitiful in the sound it makes, in the way that it butts against the window, thrusting whiskers of cold air through the gaps around the frame. So I lift the sash – just a little – and let it in.

A single paw reaches through the gap. I feel it touch my leg. It is cold, but the claws aren't out – it isn't unpleasant. Then the window rattles as it crawls inside, pushing the glass against the frame. For a moment it curls about me, and then, in one bound, leaps across the room.

Outside it sounded like a tiger, but inside it is like a kitten – curious; exploring. It jumps from shelf to chair to dresser. It bats a hanging jumper with a paw; ruffles the pages of a book with a lick of its tongue; sends a single pencil rolling off the edge of the bedside table.

It rubs its cheek possessively across the corner of the dresser, the bookcase, the edge of the bedspread; and I smell the scent of it – raindrops, open skies, and night air. I want to bury my fingers in its coat; to grab hold and let it carry me, night clothes flapping, out into the sky – leaping from rooftop to rooftop, from tree branch to cloud edge and beyond. But it is growing restless, threatening to tumble the precious things off the bookshelves as it turns.

I put a bowl of milk down in the darkness of the hallway. The wind laps at the surface, making ripples, but doesn't drink. Instead it paces this way and that, leaving cold paw prints on the carpet. Its lashing tail, winding back towards the window, sets the tasseled curtain swinging.

I reach down, hand spread, to brush my fingertips along its back, but it twists away from me, wind-quick, and is gone – banging through the open window and out. I hear it one last time as I close the window, skittering on the tiles and purring through the eaves above me.

Then it howls off into the night sky, and I go back to bed.

K

… is for Kidnappers

Insomniac

I am wandering along a street in the dark. It is deep in the night. The roads are deserted, no cars, no people. All the lights in the houses are out. I am the only thing moving, and I have no idea what I am doing here.

I have no sense of anything before this moment. I haven't been asleep — I'm dressed, walking, alert — it's more like my brain was switched off, and then suddenly on again. It's a deeply unsettling feeling, and suddenly I'm frightened of everything around me.

I look around frantically, trying to work out where I am. It is just an average suburban street, but I don't recognise it. It could be somewhere near my house, for all I know. In the still darkness everything looks different. At the far end of the road a set of traffic lights cycle pointlessly from red to green and back again.

I feel exposed. Danger could come from anywhere. The house to my left has an open front yard, and I duck into it, taking shelter behind a scraggly privet hedge. Behind me are huge black front windows, opening onto a living room — they make me think of the empty eye sockets of a skull. Nervously, I press my face against the glass and try to see something inside that will make sense of where I am, but I can only make out a few items of furniture, and a closed door, dimly illuminated by the streetlights behind me. There is no one there.

When I see the door, a memory surfaces.

I was lying in bed not sleeping. Yet another round of

insomnia had kept me drained but awake for days on end, until I'd ended up lying on the bed half dressed, staring at the ceiling.

Then, a noise – something out of place that had me fully awake in an instant. I sat bolt upright on the edge of the bed, scanning the darkness. What had it been? The noise had come from the other side of the bedroom door. Was something in the house!?

I opened the door with trembling hands, then felt stupid, because there was no one there. In the hall a piece of paper was lying on the floor by the letterbox. Had that been there before? I didn't think so. Who was putting things through my door in the middle of the night?

Frightened again, I slid into the hall, trying to stay low. I stretched out one hand for the paper and bang! something slammed against the door! Again; bang! Someone was knocking on the door, loud enough to wake the dead. I froze, then bolted for the safety of the hallway corner, shoving the paper into my pocket.

The knocking stopped and there was silence. Then, with horrible slowness, a hand slid through the letterbox. It was deathly pale, and I realised that it was wearing a white latex glove. The hand groped blindly for the lock; tested the door handle; felt along the wall. On the other side of the door something sniffed and snuffled, like a hunting dog searching for prey. It was a nightmarish noise, and I shrank into myself; but the sound stopped, and the hand withdrew, as slowly as it had come.

And then a different noise … a buzzing …

That was where the memory ended. Who had been at my door? What was the noise I'd heard? How had I got from my hallway to the street? I had no answers.

I had a thought, though. I rummaged in my pockets and pulled out the paper, then flattened it against the cold glass of the window. A message had been scrawled on it in pencil. It said "SAVE THE SLEEPERS!" and then under that a strange symbol, like an open eye inside a triangle.

I remember a horror movie I once saw. There had been an outbreak of plague in a tower block. The authorities had sealed all the doors, so that they could evacuate the people one by one, but the people inside didn't know what was happening, so they fought back, escaped, and let the disease out. Is that what is happening? Am I the rogue patient? I picture the gloved hand blindly pawing at my door – I don't think that was a doctor.

The front yard suddenly feels as unsafe as the open street did. I need to get away. Before I know it, I am running along the road, looking for an open door, a shop, a phone box, anything. Then I turn a corner, and stop short.

About a hundred yards down the street a vehicle is parked by the side of the road. It looks like a steampunk version of a flat-bed truck. A steam-train boiler is perched at the front, belching smoke from a shiny black chimney pipe. Behind the enclosed cab four huge cast iron wheels surround the open trailer, which is piled high with white sacks. The whole thing trembles as if it is alive.

I bolt for cover behind a parked car before someone sees me, just in time as it turns out. Two figures emerge from the house behind the steam-truck, carrying something between them. They are wearing long white smocks, and have what look like gas masks covering their faces. They come round the back of the truck and heave the thing they are carrying onto the trailer, and I feel sick as realise that it is a body wrapped in white plastic. They are all bodies!

I must have gasped out loud, because the two figures look up from their work, staring directly at the parked car. I can't stay here, whatever they are I don't want them to find me, so I run back for the corner.

I can hear their heavy feet on the tarmac behind me, they

are chasing me! But they are hobbled by boots, smocks, masks. I'm faster – or I hope I am. The empty streets offer no shelter. I just pray I can lose them somewhere in the back alleys and lanes, so I duck into the first opening I can see, hoping that it isn't a dead end.

I find myself in an enclosed lot. It's almost pitch black, and I am surrounded by high garden walls topped with broken glass. There are doorways in the walls, but it's too dark for me to make out what is in them, and I rebound off closed doors, scrabbling my way from one to another in desperation.

Then I see that someone has scrawled the eye mark on one of the doors with chalk. I don't stop to question. I wrench open the door and slam it behind me, putting my back against it.

I'm in someone's back garden. A narrow path leads away from the door, vanishing into the darkness. I could run up the path, but I'm frozen with fear again. I don't dare move from the door in case it opens again and those gloved hands get me.

The pursuing footsteps slow to a stop somewhere in the yard behind the door, and I hear that horrible snuffling again. It grows closer, moves away again, stops, moves on, and I realise that they are checking each door in turn. I have to move, but I can't. Instead I kneel on the damp path and press an eye to a crack in the door.

One of the figures is standing just a few feet away. Now that I am close to him, I can see that it isn't a gas mask he is wearing, but a plague doctor's mask made of brown leather, with a long dropping beak and flat black lenses for eyes. As I watch he lifts the mask up a little with one latex covered hand and sniffs the air, casting back and forth after some invisible scent. He drops the mask back into place and turns towards the door. I am sure he'll notice the mark, but the blank gaze slides past as if he can't even see the door, let alone what's scrawled on it, and he moves out of sight.

I stay where I am for a long time, thinking furiously. Who are these people? I have no answer for that, move on. What are they doing? Taking people out of their houses, putting them in their vehicle. Is everyone dead? I peer at the note again: 'SAVE THE SLEEPERS'. Could they just be asleep instead of dead? So deeply asleep that these — call them plague doctors — can just carry them away? If so, why am I not in the back of that truck with all the rest of them? But of course I don't sleep, not when I'm deep in the grip of the insomnia. Is that the answer? That I just didn't fall asleep when everyone else did? It's a working theory.

The cold is seeping into my body, now that I'm not moving, and my legs are cramping up from crouching against the door, but I push those things out of my mind and focus on the puzzle, because it keeps me from thinking about how scared I am.

So the doctors come and put everyone to sleep, but I don't sleep. And somebody knows this, because they put the note through my door. Whoever it is, they are depending on me to save everyone else, which is crazy. And they are marking safe places for me to hide.

The thought makes me stare into the blackness of the garden again. Is the person who left the note hiding out there, in amongst the bushes? If I call out, will they hear me? I don't dare call out.

If I believe all this, then I have a decision to make. I can stay where I am till morning, and hope that this all goes away, or I can go back to the steam-truck and try to do something. Staying where I am is very attractive, but it isn't an option. What if the note-writer isn't out there? What if it there is no one else to help but me? If I wait till morning the doctors and their cargo will both be gone.

I don't know if one or both of the doctors is still in the yard, so I creep the other way, up the garden path to the house beyond. The back door of the house isn't locked, but I still feel like a burglar as I move down the hall. I glance through each doorway in turn, hoping to see the mysterious stranger who will explain it all to me, but there is no one there. It's going to have to be me after all. Luckily the front door is unlocked, and I let myself nervously back out into the street.

The steam truck is where I left it. Two doctors are on their way down the street, letting themselves into a house through the front door. Are they the same pair as before? I have no idea.

I'd love to take a moment to gather my courage, but there is no time. Instead I hurry to the back of the truck, eyes flicking every which way for danger. Close up it's huge. It smells of hot oil and antiseptic. Looking up I can see dozens of wrapped up bodies. They are stacked around some sort of humming electrical device. A metal rod, supporting a copper arial shaped like an eye inside of a pyramid.

I clamber into the trailer and grab the nearest body. The wrapping isn't plastic, like I thought, but something like layers of spiderweb, tough but tearable. The body inside is breathing softly, and when I rip open the covering I even recognise her — she's the brunette who mans the convenience store checkout in the afternoons.

I shake her, slap her, shout into her ear, but she's dead to the world. Nothing I do wakes her. Desperately I try another person, and another; they are stacked up on top of each other like cordwood, men, women, even children. I clamber on top of them, trying to drag them off the platform, but it's pointless.

I give up. I'm hyperventilating. I know that the doctors will come back and catch me at any moment. What did the author of the note expect me to do? The only thing I have going for me is that I didn't fall asleep; and what good is that now? Save the sleepers — how for Christ's sake!

Then it hits me — the mark on the bottom of the note. I thought it was just to indicate safety, but it looks just like the buzzing device planted in the middle of all the bodies. What am I? I'm the insomniac, and these people need to wake up. If that thing is keeping them asleep, maybe I can use it to wake them up. It's crazy, but then this whole thing is crazy.

I start climbing. Behind me I hear feet pounding down the road, but I ignore them. I'm using the sleeping bodies as footholds. It's horrible, but I get to the top before the doctors get to me, and grab the metal of the arial with both hands. It burns me, but I hang on. I don't know what to do, but I try to channel all the sleeplessness in my body into it, all the whirling thoughts and churning anxieties that keep me awake night after night. Wake up! Wake up!

For a moment I'm sure it hasn't worked. Then the pile of bodies under my feet shifts. People start to move. They rip their way sleepily out of their cocoons and stager to their feet. Their eyes are blank, like sleepwalkers, I don't think they know what's happening.

The doctors are still trying to get to me, but the sleepers are shoving past them, and the machine is spitting sparks, but I can't focus on any of it. Everything keeping me awake, even the adrenaline fear, has poured out of my body into the sleepers, and I am so tired.

I take two steps … and fall asleep.

* * *

I wake up to the sound of birds singing. Late morning sunlight is pouring through my bedroom window. I'm lying on top of the covers in jeans and a t-shirt.

"What a crazy stupid dream," I think. Insomnia saves the world, I wish!

I sit up, and something crumples in my pocket. Of course I know at once what it is, but I don't believe it, not till I pull the note out of my pocket and see the smudged message and the eye in the pyramid.

L

… is for **Lost**

The Gap

At the start of October I accepted a job renovating an abandoned building. It was hard manual labour in an out of the way location, a bleak and lonely estate unused since the sixties, but it suited my mood – it had been three months since Hazel had left me; I was in need of distraction, but not company.

Rowlands House sat on the edge of town, a brick and wood edifice marred by later concrete additions. Behind the anonymous surrounding wall everything was dilapidated and overgrown. Tangles of willowherb rose higher than my head when I arrived, concealing heaps of rubble from some previous attempt at restoration.

Mrs Sito, who was in some way connected to the renovation project, met me on the first day, clipboard in hand, to show me around.

"Rowlands House was a printing works in the mid 18th Century," Mrs Sito told me, "for fabrics I think. Later the manor was knocked down, and the works was put to all sorts of uses: factory, workshop, then finally an office." She took me on a tour around the various outbuildings, pointing out where, over the years, people had put in garages, storerooms, flaking toilet blocks, and unidentifiable workshops.

"Of course a lot of this is coming down. These outbuildings will be demolished, and there is going to be a new driveway here," Mrs Sito tapped at items on her checklist as she spoke. "The main building is your responsibility. I'm afraid you are going to be working for your own for quite a while.

"Now, you understand about the heritage conditions?"

"Yes, of course."

Mrs Sito smiled a professional sort of smile. "Of course, of course. Well you came highly recommended Mr Finn. Let's go inside."

Rowlands House was my first project since I set up business on my own; I needed it to work, so I paid careful attention to the tour. There was a lot to be done. Someone had spent far too much time covering the original brickwork in crumbling plasterboard and artex, and the detritus of the abandoned office was heaped up everywhere in drifts of 60s junk.

After Mrs Sito left, the place was almost eerily silent. The infrequent traffic was muffled, and no one passed by the rusting gates on foot. It was easy to imagine that the outside world had vanished.

I wandered through the empty rooms. It was a maze of a place. Looking carefully I could see the beauty of the old house under the accretions of junk. The narrow stairs to the second floor were probably as old as the building, and when I pulled aside a corner of the old plasterboard I could see traces of the decorative brickwork underneath. I was surprised to see the original lead piping still in place. It would have to be replaced, and the wiring too, but that was a job for other specialists. My responsibility was stripping the place back to its historical roots.

Over the following days I set to work with gusto, ripping out the dilapidated fixtures to reveal the old house underneath. I set myself up a base of operations in a nearby outbuilding where the power was still connected. With a kettle for tea, and work lights placed around the ground floor, it started to feel like home, even when the nights drew in early. Somehow the place never seemed sinister to me, although I am sure it would have done to many; if anything it seemed ephemeral — as if my demolition work might remove the whole thing by accident. I laughed it off and turned up the volume on my portable radio, but the feeling remained.

I began to worry that my subconscious was trying to warn me about some subsidence or instability that I had noticed but not registered, so I downed tools for a day to conduct a thorough survey. This time I didn't just wander the rooms, I combed them from top to bottom, checking roof, walls, and floors for any telltale signs. I even climbed up the rickety wooden ladder that led onto the steeply tiled rooftop. Balancing on the pitch of the roof I felt more isolated than ever, closer to the grey rafts of cloud above than I was to the distant city.

I've always had a head for heights, but for some reason the roof of Rowlands House made me scared. I felt that the dark bulk of the house was collapsing beneath me, as if it was being sucked away into an unseen space. For a terrifying moment I almost lost my footing. My head spun, the clouds took on macabre shapes, and the red tiles seemed to pulse in time with my frantic heartbeat.

I scrambled down the ladder and swore to go nowhere near that roof again without safety lines or scaffolding.

At the back of the building a narrow corridor or passage connected the main rooms to the weed strewn courtyard where the sheds and outbuildings were located. It had a door at its inner end, leading into what had once been a back office, but the other end was an open archway lined in off-white tiles. This was the route to and from my workshop, and I'd run bunches of cables along it to connect the lights in the main house.

After the incident on the roof I wanted no more of high places, and so I turned my attention to the passageway. Here, I thought, the dirty boarding might conceal original tiles, like the few that remained around the archway.

By the end of the day I had removed all of the boards along one side of the passage — and had uncovered something strange.

Around the middle of the corridor, a little closer to the heart of the building than the edge, there was a gap in the wall. It was an impossible gap, I could see that at once. It was a little less than five feet high, and probably no more than three wide, but I could see at least fifteen feet of ragged tunnel extending away within it. It should have opened straight onto the back office, or possibly into the little network of storerooms tucked away behind the stairs, but it did not — it went somewhere … else.

I went straight round to the other side of the wall; I made measurements; I tapped the brickwork; I rubbed my eyes and worried that my experience on the roof was a sign of impending madness. There was no way that the gap opened into the rest of the building.

Back in the hallway I examined the opening by the fading sunlight. It was shaped a little like an open mouth, with ragged bricks for teeth jutting up each side. When I shone a torch through the opening I could see a tunnel of jumbled brickwork, layer upon layer of it, dwindling into the distance.

I hesitated on the threshold. Going in was crazy, but how could I not?

I had to crouch to make my way into the gap — the ceiling was as irregular as the walls. There was junk everywhere: manilla envelopes, crumpled papers, skeins of greying rubber bands, roofing tiles and plaster boards, loose bricks and crockery. The beam of my torch picked out curls of cloth, and wooden printing blocks lodged in crannies. It was as if the shed skin of Rowlands House had been sucked into the gap over the years and forgotten.

I wanted to go further, to find out how deep the rabbit hole led, but my torch was flickering, dimming in and out. I tapped it against my hand — I knew the battery was fresh — and it went out for a heart-stopping moment before stuttering back to life.

I got out of there.

By the time I returned to the courtyard it was already dark. Distant streetlights cast yellow shadows on the flat clouds overhead. I saw no one. When I drove my van back into town the streets were as empty as the abandoned rooms of Rowlands House, and I was seized by the irrational fear that, in uncovering the gap, I had somehow wiped everyone else off the face of the earth. I drove with my hands clenched on the wheel, and didn't relax until I started to see people passing by; then I laughed at my own stupidity.

Back in the silence of my rented flat I considered phoning Mrs Sito, but what would I say? If I told her there was a crack in a structural wall as big as myself she would panic about subsidence. If I told her it led to a mysterious passageway, she'd find someone more sane to do the work and I'd never know what it was. Now that I'd recovered from my panic I was determined to solve the mystery on my own.

But when I went to bed the terror returned full force. I was seized by the feeling that everything around me was crumbling; dissolving into loose bricks and worm rotted wood; vanishing under creeping roots and broken concrete. I found myself grasping for the photo that lay face-down on the bedside table — the photo of Hazel and me. It wasn't her I craved, but the touch of a familiar object. When I finally managed to sleep my dreams were full of disconnected rooms. I was lost deep in the passageway, stuffing mementos of my relationship into a builder's wheelbarrow.

The next morning I rose early and drove back to Rowlands through the quiet morning streets. I approached the gap armed with a heavy work torch, freshly charged, and a backup lamp clamped to my hard hat. I wore sturdy overalls, and looped a length of light rope between my waist and a tie-off in the corridor. I probably looked like a caver, and ridiculous, but I felt prepared.

That day I delved far deeper than before. I passed through grottoes and caverns of victorian brick which were choked with heaps of discarded paperwork, like some sort of giant packrat's burrow. I picked my way through stacks of carbon copies, then typescript, then handwritten papers.

The further I went the more things fell apart. The once solid brick walls became rotten and full of holes. Loose bricks covered the ground, then brick dust, then nothing but the finest sheen of sand.

At last the passage opened up, not into the cave or chamber I'd expected, but what appeared to be outside. Only it was not any outdoors I recognised. The sky, if that's what it was, was the colour of milk and luminous. A pale and directionless light that was hard to look at. The floor – the word ground seemed wrong – was perfectly level and faintly grey; flat, and with the texture of polished concrete.

Stacks of brickwork littered the plain, like islands in a flat sea. Some were no more than loose heaps, others were chunks of walls, fragments of arches, sections of supporting pillars, seemingly transported here at random from a dozen different buildings.

Again I wanted to go deeper, but now I was at the limit of my safety rope, and I didn't want to go on without it. It wasn't that I was afraid, as such – what I had found was too bizarre to understand as fear – but that I didn't want to get lost in this expanse.

My third expedition, later that day, went further. Some contractor had left a set of surveyor's equipment – ranging poles and prism levels – in one of the front rooms of the House, so I brought them with me. Although it was hard work to manoeuvre them through the narrow spaces, I could use them to navigate.

When I returned to the lambent plain I set up marker

poles behind me as I wandered. It was totally quiet, even my footsteps were muffled. No echoes. Something to do with entropy? I thought of a deserted beach in winter and imagined I could hear the sea, but it was only the blood rushing in my ears.

Although I thought that I was wandering at random, I became aware that I was following in someone else's tracks. Faint footprints marked the sandy floor — they must have been there since the 70s at the latest, maybe earlier.

The footprints ended at a gap between two rearing piles of stone, like the plinths of a broken arch. Framed between them was a vast pale shape, like the shadow of a skyscraper, far enough in the distance that all detail was reduced to a blue-grey smudge. Here, someone had written a message, painting it on the smooth concrete ground with what I took to be printer's ink, because it was thick and shiny like pitch.

In broad letters it said, "As you love life, go back, cover the gap, save yourself!" and it was signed 'M Hickert'.

The sight of the warning snapped me out of whatever strange self-hypnosis I had been suffering. Suddenly I was aware that I was standing in an impossible place, a place where someone else had come and fled in terror. I was surrounded by the remnants of my own world, which had apparently been swallowed and inexorably broken up. The vast tunnel behind me was like a gullet connecting to the gap.

What was happening back there? What had I done?

I backed away from the arch and the shadow. For an awful minute I couldn't work out which way was out, but then I spied the winking light of a ranging pole. I hadn't gone too far, not yet.

I scrambled out of the gap into the chill of early evening. The whole day had slipped by unnoticed — what else had the gap swallowed!?

I was as frightened as I had been the night before, but

there were no familiar things to comfort me. I wandered the grounds of Rowlands House in a daze. The outbuildings looked like cardboard cutouts, without substance, and the tangles of willowherb seemed as white as the sky beyond the gap. Beyond the surrounding wall everything was hidden. I didn't dare go out of the gates to see if the world was still there.

In a frantic state I grabbed wood from the yard and nailed it over the gap. I was convinced that every moment it was uncovered more of the world would vanish!

Afterwards I thought, if other people had entered the gap before me, then it had been uncovered before. If it had been uncovered before, then uncovering it wasn't the end of the world.

Reassured by my logic I dared the gates, and saw to my relief that the distant outline of the city was just as before. I had found something inexplicable, yes, but there was no need for panic. My fear was simply the product of shock. As for the warning scrawled within the gap, well surely 'M Hickert', whoever he or she was, had been irrationally scared in just the same way. If I could just keep my nerve I could solve the mystery of Hickert, and the gap.

A few weeks before, Mrs Sito's assistant had paid me a visit, bringing with him a treasure trove of historical documents that they hoped might help with the restoration. I had stored them in the front office, occasionally referring to the 1950s plan drawings as I worked. Now I took the whole bundle to my workshop and laid it out on the long trestle table. With the door fastened and the radio tuned softly to a music station, it was easy to block out any thought of the gap and concentrate on the documents.

There was no mention of a Hickert amongst the various typewritten staff lists from the House's time as an office building, so I turned instead to the earliest papers. Here were etched elevations of the old house, meticulous copperplate accounts, bills of sale, and orders of work from the time of George the Second. Amongst these I found the name of Morton Hickert, who for a period had been master of Rowlands Hall – what we now called the house.

Hickert had been the genius behind the printing works, an artist with the woodblock who had brought the French technique up from Surrey. He had persuaded the Rowlands to finance the works in 1823, and had vanished one night in 1830.

Vanished? It seemed that Morton Hickert's fate was a mystery. Some claimed he had been murdered, others that he had fled the country with a fortune in money he owed to the Rowlands. To me it seemed clear that he had entered the gap and never returned.

But the gap could not have remained open for centuries. Something must have happened to it. I returned to the yellowing papers in search of answers, and eventually found a record of building work conducted in the same year as Hickert's disappearance. The House had been damaged by a storm, it said, and urgent repairs to the fabric had been required, including the addition of new panelling in both the front office and the rear passage.

Now I had a record of events. The gap had existed even in Hickert's day. Perhaps it had appeared only then, or perhaps it had been growing unnoticed till that point. After Hickert had vanished, the gap had been mistaken for storm damage and covered over. This could not be the full story, however. The boarding I had pulled down had not been 18th century elm, but 1950s plywood. Sometime later the old panelling had been torn down and replaced. That, surely, must have been when the twentieth century junk had entered. That meant that the gap had been revealed at least twice, and both times the world had survived. Nothing was going to disintegrate; my fears were meaningless.

By the small hours of the morning I had convinced myself, despite all the evidence of my eyes, that the gap was safe. When I slipped into the sleeping bag spread out against the back wall of the workshop, I slept the sleep of the just — easy and without dreams. Tomorrow, I told myself, I would take photos; make notes; prepare to reveal my discovery to the world.

The next morning I studied the gap by sunlight. The hastily erected boards I had nailed up the previous night barely served to cover it. A wide chink lay uncovered on the right, and the top of the crack appeared to extend through the roof of the corridor into the second floor.

Had I mis-remembered the size? No. Had I positioned the board badly in my panic? Surely not. There could be no doubt that the gap had grown larger. When I bent close to the corridor wall I could see hairline cracks extending through the old plaster, marking out the edges of the invisible brickwork, and I imagined that I could hear the gentle scrape of bricks falling from their places behind the board.

What was causing it? What did it mean? I was convinced that the answers to my questions could only lie inside the gap, and I had persuaded myself that looking for them would do no harm.

Once again I stooped my way through the winding passage; once again I followed my marker poles to the broken arch and Hickert's mysterious warning, but this time I passed through and headed across the open whiteness, following the trail of footprints towards what I was sure was the heart of the mystery.

Time passed. I could not say how much. It might have been hours, or even days. There was nothing in that place which could have helped me measure it. I tried to fix my eyes on a landmark and measure progress that way, but the plain became emptier and emptier. As for the shadow tower, if that's what it was, is retreated before me as fast as I approached.

Eventually I could go no further. My legs ached, and my

body felt as if it was fading away under me. There was nothing there; the shadow was no closer. I sunk exhausted to the ground, letting the heavy sighting pole fall beside me, and rested my head in my hands. I no longer felt elated at the thought of reaching the heart of the gap, instead I worried that there was no heart, only this endless dissolving place. I tried not to imagine the house falling, brick by brick, into the emptiness behind me.

When I opened my eyes I saw that I was not alone.

A little way from where I sat a section of wall, like the base of a monument, had emerged from the glare. It was perhaps twelve feet high and a little less in width, surrounded by a drift of detritus that had fetched up against it as if blown by the wind. Seated beside the mound of rubbish was the body of a man, dressed in what I took to be Georgian clothing – Morton Hickart.

Hickart looked like he had stopped to take a rest and simply never moved again. He sat with his back to the wall, his head leaning back. He looked like the mummies I had sometimes seen on TV – his flesh was hard and tight like old leather, turned grey by the powder sand. His lips had drawn back from his teeth, but his eyes were closed underneath the grey tresses of his wig. A canvass satchel by his side crumbled to dust when I touched it, revealing fragments of brushes and paper, desiccated ink, and a brass telescope. I was lost; the footsteps led nowhere.

There were other things fetched up against the wall that scared me even more than the corpse of Hickert: faded floral curtains that reminded me of the ones my mother used to have; broken tools that I swear had come from my workshop; a headless floppy doll just like the one I lost as a boy; and worst of all, a picture frame, face down.

I lifted the picture frame with trembling fingers, hoping that it was not the picture of Hazel that should have been beside my bed – but of course it was.

I didn't run out, not that time. I knew what I was going to find. All my self-deceptions were exposed; the gap was not safe. While I had played at explorer, the world inside the gap had quietly reached out and destroyed my own — the picture proved it. Instead I wandered, aimless, ignoring my own markers. Somehow, without meaning to, I found myself back at the passage, and mechanically returned up it as I had before.

When I emerged from Rowlands House the outbuildings were gone. Nothing but empty concrete patches, free of weeds, showed that they had ever existed. The iron gates led onto empty streets, without cars, without lights, without people. When I put the faint glow of the work-lights behind me and stared out into the darkness I could see nothing. There were no buildings, no city lights, just a haze that might be mist. When I tried to place a call to Hazel, to Mrs Sito, to anyone, I got nothing on my phone but a hiss of static.

I returned to the gap — where else could I go. The House, which was the only structure left, was beginning to disintegrate too. Each time I wandered desperately back in, and then despairingly back out, the outside world fragmented further. By the third or fourth return, the sky over Rowlands House had become the same flat and luminous white as the sky within. It was all one.

I didn't know then what I had done that had finally drawn the world into the gap, and I still don't. Had I left the crack uncovered longer then before? Had I simply hastened the last part of a long process? Had I broken some precarious balance when I went too far and came back? Was it my fault? How long till I went the way of Morton Hickert?

And the final question, the one I keep asking myself as I sit with my back against the last fragment of Rowlands House — have I really destroyed the world, or simply myself? Maybe there really is nothing, anywhere, any more; but maybe, just maybe, the world is going on its way as it always has somewhere out there – the only difference being that I am missing from it.

I truly hope so.

M

… is for **Mirror**

Solomon's Gate

When Solomon Morton first acquired Widow's Chase, it was a small country manor in the vernacular style, which had stood unchanged in the middle of its modest parkland for the previous 180 years. Morton's arrival was quickly followed by a veritable frenzy of building, as he set about converting the chase into a gothic fantasy. Craftsmen were brought over specially from the continent, at a cost (his neighbours presumed) that must have dwarfed the purchase price of the manor itself.

Under Morton's personal direction, along with that of an Italian architect named Martello, the original house was encased in a facade of cream coloured sandstone, the most prominent feature of which was a mock belfry, or gatehouse, three stories high. This tower was faced with elaborate arabesques and bas reliefs in the neoclassical style: nymphs and oneiropomps, mnemosynes and hypnos, all arranged according to some occult design; and containing within it an equally ornate gate.

The building work, which continued well after Solomon Morton took possession of the house, excited much comment (little of it good), in the local area, as did the strange gatherings over which Morton presided. These house parties, which were often a week long, featured occultists of all sorts: London spiritualists, Indian fakirs, Scandinavian theosophists, and dissolute artists. Their noise, flamboyant behaviours, and outrageous appearances, shocked Solomon Morton's neighbours, who whispered that

Morton was involved in something diabolic, and matters might well have come to an unpleasant confrontation, had Morton not been suddenly, and unexpectedly, found dead outside the front door of the house.

Upon Solomon's death the Chase was almost instantly abandoned. His outré friends vanished, his sculptors downed tools, his workmen returned to the continent, and the majority of the servants rapidly found new situations, amidst rumours that the house was haunted. It soon transpired that the majority of Morton's fortune was also gone, and that his estate was burdened with complex debts. (At which news the parish Doctor, Rowlands, suggested darkly that Morton's Satanic dabblings had taken their toll.)

For three years the house was mired in tortuous legal battles, until eventually one William Hickert found himself inheriting it; which is where our story properly begins.

William had only a tenuous relation to the Morton family, and none at all to Solomon, an uncle many times removed of whom he had never heard. He had completed a tour of the continent some years before, and had made a tolerable living in London as an editor for an academic magazine, but his health had suffered, growing worse with every day he remained in the capital. It had long been the opinion of William's doctor that he should move to the country, and the sudden arrival of Widow's Chase seemed like a godsend.

So it was that, early in October, William Hickert arrived at Widow's Chase as its new resident. The oak trees were turning brown, and the sky was the pale blue of autumn. In the clear light the house looked strangely etherial, with its unfinished tower reaching skyward.

The sole resident when he arrived was Minwell, the butler, who had remained at his post throughout the years of legal wrangling. Minwell met him at the front gate, conveyed him up the long path beneath the oaks, and showed him to his rooms, which were on the same side of the house as the tower.

William had been struck by the baroque nature of the outside of the house – by the statues, the flying buttresses, and the gothic arches – so he was pleasantly surprised to discover that the interior was comfortably human in scale, with small white rooms and exposed beams. His new bedroom, for example, was so quaintly proportioned that he found it hard to believe he was even in the same house.

"If you'll forgive me sir," said Minwell, "it is my opinion that the old master had far more building in mind, that was never completed."

"Opinion Minwell? Weren't you around when the plans were drawn up then?"

"Oh no sir! The truth is that I was only in Master Morton's service for a few months before his death."

William dearly wanted to ask more about the circumstances of Solomon Morton's death, but Minwell remained silent on the subject, and soon a plethora of urgent practical matters served to distract him from it.

Over the course of the following weeks William was kept busy supervising the transfer of his property to the Chase, the re-opening of the grounds, and the tricky business of securing new servants, since none of his own had followed him from London. He had many books, and spent much of his time in Solomon Morton's oak-panelled library, trying to make room for his own volumes amongst the many obscure and occult tomes.

It was around this time that William first became troubled by a recurring dream. He had often been a poor sleeper, and put it down to the disturbance of sleeping in a new bed in a new house, till one day he awoke with a particularly vivid recollection of the nightmare.

He had been standing in a long and dimly lit corridor. The walls were dark oak, and ribbed like the vault of a cathedral. To either side of him were the open halves of an enormous gate, which were as pale as ivory. The gate thronged with figures, and it seemed to him that they writhed, and tried to speak; though they made no noise.

There was light behind him; and ahead, at the far end of the passage, was an answering glimmer, like a reflection in a mirror. In the fashion of dreams he walked the length of the corridor without looking back, eyes fixed on the wavering light ahead. At one moment he thought that it was a pool of water fixed to the wall, at another a full length Cheval Glass that had once stood in his parent's house, but finally it settled into the familiar shape of a wardrobe with a mirrored door.

The mirror was grey and dim, as if the silvering had all but worn away, and his reflection was also grey and dim, like a drowned man beneath water. Horribly, the creature reflected in the glass was not him. It was like him, but changed, in a way that his dreaming mind could not grasp, and the very sight of it terrified him. It was this sensation – of the face in the mirror not quite being his own – which continued to unsettle him after waking.

The next morning William mentioned the dream to Minwell during breakfast.

"I had the most curious dream last night, Minwell. There was a passage, and the most peculiar gate, all covered in figures."

"Oh yes sir," Minwell nodded sagely, "Solomon's Gate."

"You know of it?"

"Of course sir, it is on the property, after all."

This statement amazed William, who was certain that he had never heard of Solomon's Gate before, but he was mollified by the suggestion that he had, perhaps, seen it in one of Morton's books without being fully aware of it.

"I have the keys here sir, if you wish to look."

The gate, naturally enough, was located in the gatehouse, that fantastical and oppressive tower which William had not yet got around to visiting.

Minwell led him out of the house, and round to the unfinished tower by means of a small path, which terminated at a pair of plain wooden doors set into a gothic arch, above which was situated a curious statue — a blind man pouring water.

These doors were large enough to admit a cart, and ought to have led to a courtyard, or other open space. Instead, when the doors were unlocked and opened, William found himself in a curious vaulted grotto of a chamber, similar in size and shape to the porch of a church, which occupied the entire lower level of the tower.

Within this chamber was a second, blind, arch, set into the back wall, and in front of that, the gate.

William's first impression was of a mass of complex and decorative metalwork that resembled the gates of a crypt. Figures of women with their heads bowed and their eyes covered by their hands flanked curlicues of greenery, poppy flowers, jugs of water, rivers, branches. Unlike the gate in his dream this gate did not shine white, but was cast from some dull metal resembling lead. Behind the gate, separated from it by about a foot of space, was a solid wall onto which a sheet of polished bronze had been fixed. With a shock Williams realised that the wall must back onto the very part of the house where his room was located.

"In my dream the gate was white."

"I do believe, sir, that the intention was to cover the gate with ivory or horn, but the work was never completed. The sculptor, Martello, was one of the first to leave on the old master's death."

William looked around the gloomy vault, with its half-finished carvings, and faceless figures, and was reminded uncomfortably of the hazy face he'd seen in the dream.

"I don't like this place," he said, surprised by his own candour.

"If I may sir, I believe it was this room in particular that the other servants disliked."

"Disliked?"

"There were suggestions that it was haunted."

William made a dismissive noise, but he ordered Minwell to lock the doors and put away the keys.

After his visit to the tower, William spent some days ensconced amongst Solomon Morton's papers, searching for plans of the house. He wanted some sort of explanation that might explain its bizarre construction. For three days he barely left the library, but all he had to show at the end were a handful of esoteric sketches in Morton's hand. There had been other drawings, of that he was sure, but they were not in the house. Eventually a ledger drawn up by Morton's solicitor provided the answer – the plans and architectural drawings had been taken by Martello. At once William took up pen and ink and put his rusty Italian to the test writing a letter to the sculptor.

It was only when he finished that he looked at the letter and said to himself, "I am becoming obsessed".

William made sure the letter was posted, and then made an effort to distance himself from both the dreams and the house. It was by now mid-November, but the weather was unseasonably clear and bright, perfect for visiting, and William took the time to make the acquaintance of his neighbours. For the space of two weeks he lunched and dined at the various manor houses and halls of the area, and though he was still troubled by dreams of the gates, he was in good spirits.

It was during this period that William encountered Rowlands, the parish Doctor. The two hit it off, despite the Doctor's dire pronouncements about Widow's Chase and its former inhabitants. It was from Rowlands that William finally learnt the questionable rumours about Morton and his shocking parties, and it was to Rowlands alone (excepting Minwell) that he disclosed his disquieting dreams.

"It puts one in mind of the gates of horn and ivory," opined the Doctor, as the two of them took tea one blustery late November day, in the sitting room overlooking the Doctor's garden.

"The portals of dreams, if I remember my Homer, at the entrance to the house of Hypnos. Curious that, I do believe there's a statue of Hypnos above the doors of your tower."

"Hypnos! Of course! I wonder ..."

At this outburst the Doctor grew serious. "If I were you, I would not delve too far into Solomon Morton's madness."

"I will not!"

William meant what he said, but events were to take a different turn. That very night he dreamt again of the gloomy passage with its sepulchral gates, and its distant mirror. Once again he found himself standing before a reflecting glass (this time of polished bronze), and once again beheld a reflection that was not quite his own.

Only this time the figure did not stay a reflection. Pale hands extended through the bronze, as if it was only the surface of a reflecting pool, and grasped his own. Their grip was obscenely strong. Desperately William struggled to free himself, but could not. The hands pulled him closer, until his cheek was pressed against the cold metal, separated from that hideous face only by the slightest distance. And that face! It ran and shifted like wax! It became his own!

The maid discovered him the next day, gripped in the throws of a delirious fever, which lasted three days, and demanded a recovery of as many weeks, during which William was unable to leave the house.

Isolated within the Chase's gothic walls William gave in to his obsessions. His days were spent in the library, with a shawl around his shoulders and a mountain of occult books on every side; while at night he tossed and turned his way through jumbled dreams of gates, passages, and faceless men. He covered every mirror in the house with sheets or blankets, and filled notebooks with scribbled designs. Eventually he grew too weak even for the daily trips to the library, and demanded that the books were brought to him in bed instead.

Dreams, he thought, were the key. He was convinced that his dreams were were intimately connected with some scheme of Solomon Morton's, and that if he could understand them, the dreams and their dire portents might end. If only he had the plans to the house, but Martello had taken those.

One late December day, when the snow lay thick on the grounds, and the clouds seemed set to descend and scrape the gatehouse tower, Minwell collected a letter from the postman and brought it to his master, who was now at his customary location in his bed, surrounded by papers and discarded books.

"A letter from London, sir."

"Give it to me! Give it to me!"

William tore open the letter, which was postmarked from Marylebone, and unfolded the single sheet within. It was signed 'Martello', and contained a single line of Italian:

> *Le porte di corno e d'avorio si aprono in entrambe le direzioni!*

William read the letter, and let out a low and mournful groan. "The gates of horn and ivory open both ways," he whispered, and then cried out, "Oh God! I'm lost!"

Shocked, Minwell made to go for the Doctor, but instead William leapt out of the bed, flinging books and notes aside in his haste to rise.

"Enough of this! Minwell, I've let myself languish too long. I will go to London and confront Martello, and get some clear answers! See that a carriage is arranged for tomorrow."

This was the most activity William had shown for weeks, and everyone in his household took it as a positive sign that his long illness, and the mental turmoil that had come with it, were finally over. A carriage was called for, clothes were made ready, and his papers were returned to the Library. William, meanwhile, made plans to travel to Marylbone to confront Martello and then, perhaps, to visit his Solicitor, with an idea towards freeing himself of Widow's Chase and its turbulent dreams once and for all.

But that night, the dream. Again the gates, again the mirror, again the terrifying struggle against the thing that wore his face. When the figure laid its hands upon him he tried to pull away as before, but he was weak from his long convalescence. He could not escape it. He could not prevent it from pulling him against the glass, and this time into it!

"My dreams are my own!" he cried out in defiance, but the mirror closed over him without reply.

He awoke in a small, dark, unfamiliar space. Something hard and cold was pressed against his back, and something cold and hard against his front, trapping him like an insect between pages. Then, from in front of him, came the heavy sound of a door unlocking. A blinding wash of sunlight assaulted his eyes, and he saw bars. The gate! He was trapped between the gate and the mirror!

Before him was a numinous figure, barely visible in the light; dressed in his clothes, wearing his face. For one brief moment it paused to look back at him, as if recalling a half-remembered dream, and then slammed the doors.

William had only time to utter one last truncated cry, before the darkness and the mirror claimed him as their own.

Outside a carriage was drawn up, luggage was packed, and something that had dreamt of freedom began its journey to London.

N

… is for **Nightmare**

Dream Diary

Day ?

They are all around me. I can hear them snuffling on every side, but I can't see them. The sheets are tangled, the duvet stifling, I cannot move. There is a weight on my chest, my feet – they are holding me down!

A glimpse of yellow! A flash of brown! Squirming. Squirming against my face. I can't breathe!

Not again!

You won't have me! My dreams are my own! Not again!

Down into blackness …

Day 1

Have decided to keep a dream diary. My dreams are wonderful, epic, soaring – at least I think they are – they slip through my fingers as soon as I open my eyes. It really bugs me.

I've read that keeping a notebook by your bed and writing your dreams down as soon as you wake up can really help you hang on to them. Been thinking about it a while, decided to take the plunge.

Considered getting a special journal from the bookshop, but those things are expensive, so this notebook will have to do. Note to self – panettone recipe was on the torn out pages. Got to make it easy to write dreams down, no flipping pages at 6am.

Day 2

Something about a boy, and a trip to the seaside. Mum was promising me an ice cream, but I couldn't find the queue? It was Monday morning – no that's the song playing on the radio, making me confused.

I was so sure that I'd had a wonderful dream. I could feel it when I woke up, this sort of glow, a warm feeling like I'd just sipped hot chocolate, but it was gone before I could even reach the pen to write. Then a cold emptiness – quite horrible actually.

And it is cold. The window is open, I don't remember doing that. The sun is still pale, it's foggy. I feel like something is missing.

Not the best start.

Day 2 - later

I read that you need to really catch the dream mid way through to remember it.

Day 3

I am wandering through my old house, the one I lived in with Mum and Dad, when Dad was still alive. There is an extra door in the hallway by the stairs, and it leads to a whole other wing of the house. Somehow I do not feel surprised.

When I go to the end of the corridor I find a flight of stairs that leads up to a big open living room. The furniture is all 60's orange, with a shag-pile rug and bright windows. My

Dad is sitting on a sofa with his back to me, watching that huge white TV we had when I was little.

I am so happy to see him. I run forward, shouting his name, only I can't shout, and I can't move either. He turns to look at me, but his face is a blur that I can't make out, and it's so horrible that I scream, only I can't scream either. He keeps turning to look, like a video clip on loop, and I scream each time. The TV is flickering, brown and yellow. There is something on the screen, a pair of burning eyes and something that writhes. I wake with a scream.

No. That's not right. I woke up with a smile. It was a good dream – but when I try to write it down it turns horrible. It's like the good dream got ripped away and I was left with a nightmare instead. And the bed is wet with sweat; and so am I, even though the window is open again.

I still don't remember doing that.

I guess I must have dreamt two dreams and gotten them muddled up, one over the top of another or something. It happens.

But I could have sworn …

Day 4

Did some more reading. Apparently the body knows when you are due to wake up, if it's a regular thing. Gets itself ready for waking, so your sleep is shallow. Sunlight doesn't help either. The real stuff is in the middle of the night, the long dreams, the ones that keep slipping away from me.

Tonight I'm going to try something different. I set an alarm for the middle of the night. Not when I'm really deep, you don't dream then, but if I've timed it right I should catch one of those real dark-time dreams and get it whole. Pen to hand.

Day 5

4am alarm didn't go off – stupid thing. Maybe I turned it off in my sleep? Won't make that mistake again, tonight I'm putting it on the other side of the room.

Tired today anyway. Tried to write something in the diary but my mind was empty, as if I hadn't dreamt at all. Felt adrift all day, sure they noticed it at work. I'm still going to try again though, it's the weekend anyway so I can afford to be tired.

My nose itches.

Day 5 - later

Alarm set, here we go.

Day 6

Oh! A beautiful dream! I can remember it all. So bright! Writing this in the dark, don't want to spoil it. I can still see the towers, glass and silver. The sea washed them from below, surging, like hollow breathing. Bridges, connecting everything, from tower to tower. Ours was the tallest, and at the top that living room, with the huge windows, with my Dad in it –

What was that?

Snap on the light, jumping at shadows. Nothing there, of course. But I swear I heard something, like the pitter of feet, like something brushing against the cotton of the duvet cover. Of course there is nothing there. But the bed is rumpled, the covers half off. Did I do that? And the window … the window is open again, and this time I know I closed it!

A snuffling noise. Someone clearing their nose? Horribly

it is more like an elephant noise than anything a human might make. Outside? Oh God! Did it come from under the bed? I think it came from under the bed!

I don't want to move out from under the covers and look. Suddenly I feel so tired, it would be so easy to just switch off the light and close my eyes. So easy.

But thats crazy! There's something in the room with me and I want to go to sleep?

I peel back the covers, but it's so hard. My skin is sticky. It's cold, but I'm hot. Crawl to the edge of the bed, look down, but of course there is nothing there. Nothing there.

I fall back on the bed, feeling stupid, and freeze. There is something in the corner of the room, a dark smudge in the shadow of the wardrobe. Brown and Yellow, moving, squirming …

So tired. I think I'll sleep now.

Day 6 - later

What time is it?

The sky outside the window is evening dark, the clouds under-lit by the dirty yellow glow of street lamps. There is rain falling, hissing through the open window. Is it still night? It can't be, I must have slept through the day.

All I can remember are nightmares. Screaming; running; death. A clammy touch on my face, unable to breathe. Where have all the good dreams gone? Who has taken them? I have the sudden conviction that something is here, in my house, feeding on them, sucking the dreams out of me. The thought leaves me shaking, trembling.

I must be sick!

Feet on the floor, throw on the dressing gown that hangs on the back of the chair, get out of bed. These simple things seem so hard. I stumble across the bedroom, force open the door, get out into the hallway. How can I still be so tired? I reach for the phone to call the Doctor, but I don't do it. Somehow I know that this is about my missing dreams, and what's a Doctor going to do about those?

My nose is bleeding.

The hallway carpet is soft beneath my feet. I feel like I am sinking into it. It is pulling me down! Oh God! Am I still dreaming? I try to force myself forwards but the hallway stretches out like taffy. The carpet is dragging me backwards — go to bed, go to sleep.

No! I won't do it, I won't go back! They can't have me! I have to get to the kitchen, drink something, cool this fever I must be suffering from. It's only a few steps, I can do it!

Then I see them.

Movement at the doorway, a shadow in the shadows, dirty brown and dirty yellow like the street lamps, and eyes like chips of neon, buzzing in the rain. There's one ahead of me, and one behind. I want to run, I want to fight, but they raise their hands and move their fingers and I feel so tired.

They want me to sleep.

Day ?

They are all around me, but I can't see them. Sometimes they let me wake up, but I can't move. The sheets are wet, the duvet is heavy. They are sitting on my legs, on my chest, pressing me down. There are no good dreams left — they have eaten them all — now they have started on the bad ones. Over and over again.

If I slide my eyes I can see the diary, lying beside the bed where I left it. How long ago was that? If I could just reach it, maybe I could write … maybe I could do something.

A glimpse of yellow! A flash of brown! Squirming. Squirming against my face. I can't breathe!

Not again!
You won't have me! My dreams are my own! Not again!
Down into blackness …

O

… is for **Oceanic**

Ammonite

Whitby, 1947

The market sprawled all the way up Church Lane, from the harbour side behind Tate hill, all the way to the foot of the Donkey Wynd, where the 199 steps run so steeply up to the abbey ruins that they seem more like a slipway than a street.

There were a dozen – no two dozen – different stalls, laden with things to attract every eye: crockery and linen, boot brushes and razors, brightly coloured sticks of rock and boiled sweets.

The sweet stall was surrounded by children, handing over their pennies or tugging on the sleeves of indulgent parents, eager for a handful of bonbons or sherbet lemons; but one boy pushed past with hardly a glance. His eyes were fixed on a stall squeezed up hard against the railings at the bottom of the abbey steps.

An old checked tablecloth was spread across a trestle table, the corners weighted down with flat stones from Whitby beach. The stall-holder – a jut-bearded fisherman stuffed into a heavy knitted sweater – had covered the tablecloth with treasures gathered from the coast. There were ammonites and belemnites, jet nodules and fossilised wood, mudstones imprinted with ancient leaves, and reptile bones.

The boy had eyes only for the ammonites. Perfect spirals of ancient rock in a dozen sizes. One, the fisherman's prize, was as large as a dinner plate. The boy longed to touch it, but picked up one of the cone shaped belemnites instead.

"Shilling and a half," the fisherman said offhand, his attention focussed on a tweed suited man who was examining the choicer specimens.

The boy put the belemnite down again. He had enough money in his pocket to buy it, but his heart was set on an ammonite.

A few of the ammonites had been cut in half. Their flat surfaces were polished as smooth as glass. The exposed faces revealed spirals of internal chambers, each one identical in shape to the one before, but smaller — like a series of receiving rooms leading eventually to a secret room. The boy thought that they looked like hopscotch courts.

"Those are a half-guinea each," the fisherman said, and snorted as the boy snatched his hand away.

Reluctantly the boy turned his attention to the rougher specimens whose prices he might be able to afford. There was one, about the size of his fist, that called to him. Its grey exterior was roughly knurled, like a giant's fingertip. When he picked it up, it was as heavy as lead, and cold, despite the sun warming the tabletop. Holding it made him think of ancient seas and lightless waters.

"Two and six," the fisherman said, his voice making it clear that the boy had better choose something quickly.

The boy fumbled the coins out of his pocket, they were all he had, and handed them over. "This one," he said.

The fisherman palmed the coins away, and then deftly wrapped the ammonite up in a twist of paper.

"There you go."

He might have said something more, but at that very moment a different voice called out, "There you are Billy! Time to get on," and the boy turned and rushed away.

* * *

Much later, in the chilly gloom of the family's holiday home, the boy unwrapped the ammonite and placed it carefully on the little table in the corner of his room, where a scuffed brass lamp with a cloth shade sat in a puddle of light. He was already dressed in his stripped flannel pyjamas, but he perched on the bare wooden seat and studied the fossil in the lamplight.

The stone was dark grey, flecked with gold and silver. The edge was rough, but parts of it were as smooth as if they had been polished. He knew that sometimes men broke open rocks with geological hammers, and that a fossil might be found with flaws that would allow it to be broken open, so he ran his finger along the edge, imaging that he might be able to open it up like a pocket watch and reveal the beautiful interior – but there was no flaw.

Unlike many ammonites, the boy's fossil was complete, with the mouth of the shell still visible. He pressed his thumb into the smooth depression and thought: *So old! Sixty-six million years or more! As old as dinosaurs, as old as the stone this house was built from.*

And once it would have been alive, with a face full of tentacles right where my finger is. Did it look like a nautilus, or a squid, or something else entirely?

He could have gone on like this for hours; but that creak on the stairs was surely his mother, coming to tell him to go to sleep – so he snapped off the light and hopped between the cold pressed sheets with his eyes closed. A moment later he was asleep, dreaming of ammonites.

* * *

The night was dark and full of unfamiliar noises, the creaks and pops of a strange house settling. The boy kept his eyes closed, imagining a dark sea. It lapped and gurgled its way through the chambers of the holiday home, filling each room in turn. He thought he could hear it rising up the stairway, step by step. A moment later the water was under the door; at the edge of the bed; rolling under the covers; up to the ceiling.

Something was moving in the depths of the house. It slunk through the living room, rattling the rented china on the welsh dresser. It drifted through the hallway, brushing against the coatracks and shoe stands. It uncoiled an arm into the kitchen, sending pepper pots and tea cups tumbling like startled fish.

The boy sat up in bed, listening hard. The bedroom was full of water, but somehow he could breathe — an oddity that he ignored completely, because all his attention was focussed on the thing that he knew was creeping through the house.

A rhythmic creak and clack reverberated from the stairway, and the boy knew that something was dragging its way up the stairs, wrapping its limbs around each banister in turn. He glanced at the table and saw nothing by the lamp — the ammonite was on the stairs!

On his hands and knees he peeked through the crack of the door. He could just make out the square newel post at the top of the stairs through the murk. Something long and pale wrapped its way around it — a tentacle — and the ammonite slid into view.

The great ridged shell was smooth as polished marble. Maroon, with pale cream stripes capping each ridge, so that it looked like an inverse nautilus. Somehow the ammonite had grown as enormous as a cartwheel, so that it brushed the walls of the landing as it reached the top of the stairs.

The boy ducked back behind the door and held it shut with his back, but he could feel the wood vibrate as the ammonite brushed against it. He was frightened, but at the same time he was fascinated. Ammonites had been extinct since the Cretaceous, leaving nothing behind but countless stone corpses. Who could love history and not want to see a living one?

Cautiously he stepped back and let the door swing open. The ammonite hung motionless on the other side, its arms waving like seaweed in the tide. Up close the boy could see that it had two huge flat eyes set low amongst the cluster of tentacles, and a flexing syphon underneath. Ten suckered arms were arranged around a beak of a mouth, but there were no squid-like hunting tentacles, and no nautilus-like hood.

The boy took all of this in at a glance as the ammonite surged through door, arms splaying and beak open. Even as it came for him he raised a hand, more in greeting than fear.

The ammonite shot its arms forward and closed them around the boy's upraised hand, like Adam and the squid on the Sistine chapel ceiling. At once a shock ran through its body. The great shell cracked from top to bottom, and the whole beast came apart like a cloud of ink in the water, engulfing the boy in darkness.

He blinked awake back in bed.

The pale morning sun was shining through the bedroom window, and something heavy and cold was clutched between his hands. When he cautiously opened his fingers he saw that he was holding the ammonite fossil, and that somehow – during the night – it had split in half, revealing the many chambered spiral within.

P

... is for **Prophecy**

Fortune Teller

I couldn't afford the twenty drachmas to see the Pythoness, so I went down to the market and stuck a dime in the coin operated Raven machine to get my fortune told.

The stuffed Raven whirred and rotated on its perch, pecking repeatedly at the bald spot under its wing. The red velvet lining the base of its glass dome had gone grey with dust. I fixed my eyes on the ticking iron gears that formed the Raven's perch, it doesn't do to meet an Oracle's eye.

When I finally caught the Raven's attention I submitted my question, which I'd scrawled in water on a fold of rice paper. The words had faded while I'd waited, but the Raven snapped the paper up readily enough and set about producing its answer.

I'd asked the Raven about Mickey Finn. My employers wanted to talk to Mickey about a little arson matter. By the time I'd gotten to Mickey's place he'd already flown the coop, which was something the Raven ought to have been an expert in, but when its prophecy came spooling out of the slot on four feet of paper tape it was nothing but badly printed platitudes.

"Goldfish shoals are nipping at your toes. Sow where ye plan to weep. Honour the Gods. Honour the Carneia. Beware of heights."

I directed an angry kick at the side of the machine, thinking that it served me right for choosing sub-standard oracles. The Raven flapped its wings in anger, turned a full circle, and spat out a tape that said, "Get stuffed!"

I'm used to doing the rounds of penny-ante fortune tellers when I'm on a case – generally you've got to ask a few of them before you get clear answers, which is why my clients pay me to do it rather than getting their own prophecies – but this was a particularly poor showing.

I went back to the front of the shop, intending to take my frustrations out on the proprietor, but there was no sign of the man. Rows of bubbling fish tanks were lined up along the back half of the room, each one more gaudily fluorescent than the last, with lampshades of green glass overhead. It was a good place to hide from an angry customer, so I peered between them to see if he was hiding from my wrath. I found nothing but a bug-eyed fish that stared at me through the side of its tank. I didn't like its look, so I bent down and rapped on the glass to scare it away.

To my dismay the tank tottered on its stand, rocking back and forth in response to my touch. I tried to steady it with my hand, but that only made it worse. Over it went, spraying glass, water, fish, and ornamental plants all over my freshly polished shoes.

I cursed three ways to heaven, then had a second thought. 'Goldfish shoals are nipping at your toes,' the prophecy said. Accurate or a coincidence? I decided to give the Raven the benefit of the doubt and take it as genuine, in which case I was looking for somewhere I planned to weep - or reap.

"Day's looking up," I muttered to myself, and then tucked an obol bill beside the register to cover the cost of the fish tank.

Half of my profession is happenstance and synchronicity, so I kept my eyes about me as I shouldered my way through the market crush. It was festival time, and the place was full to the gills with locals on holiday, out of town rubes, and petty thieves making a killing. If Mickey were hiding out anywhere around here he was on to a good thing. I caught sight of the aquarium owner helping himself to a paper-wrap of fried shrimp from a stall to the left, so I turned right.

Clockwork automatons with over-fat frogs in their cage-work heads were stomping their way between the fish frying stalls and the pachinko parlours. These Frog-heads had been all through the town since the start of the month, putting two drachma bets on the foot races and clogging up the waterways. On a hunch I decided to follow them.

The Frog-heads were slow and ponderous, I guess their flippers didn't handle the controls very well, so I loitered behind them for a good half an hour without seeing anything unusual. By the time we got to the bookbinders' district I was muttering choice words about the usefulness of oracles and seriously considering trying a different tack.

The lanes got narrow there, most people went single file, but the Frog-heads metal–shouldered their way through, sending flocks of mechanical finches scattering off the stall awnings. A group of scrawny finch catchers shook their fists at the automatons, but they got out of the way before it came to blows; no clues there.

I considered following the finch catchers instead, but then I caught sight of the closed doors of the temple of Demeter, which formed a backdrop to the confrontation. The olive-wood panels were marked with sheaves of grain, symbols of the harvest. A place to reap? It was worth a try.

I pushed the door open cautiously, with one hand on the pistol I'd dropped into the pocket of my coat. The inside of the temple was dark and dusty. The air was full of wheat chaff, and no one had bothered to put on the lights, so I had to navigate by what little sunlight that made it through the cracks in the shutters.

The place was full of garlands and wicker floats. I realised that these were decorations prepared for the Carneia, which was already getting started in the fields behind the market. Another word from the Raven's prophecy; and plenty of cover as well.

I went in low and fast, with the gun out. If I met a

priestess instead of Mickey it couldn't be helped. Better to have to apologise than to get shot.

Mickey still caught me nearly dead. He pushed one of the wicker men over right on top of me. I managed to get out of the way only by throwing myself to the floor. No warning from the oracle there! I took a pot shot with the gun and hit nothing but flowers. Mickey tried to stamp on my hand. I pulled my fingers out of the way just in time, but the gun went spinning off into the darkness somewhere.

Mickey whaled on me a while, while I tried my best to whale back. Luckily for me, Mickey was more of a thief than a fighter. Unluckily I was on my back and covered in flowers, which put me at something of a disadvantage. I'm more of a researcher than a brawler myself, which is why I prefer oracles to punching.

The commotion must have reached the ears of the priestesses, because we both heard the clang of the alarm gong, and knew that the hoplites would be on their way. I aimed a kick at Mickey's shins, but he was already running, tipping over half a dozen poppy covered figures as he went.

I pulled myself to my feet. There was blood on my cheek, and the knuckles on my right hand were raw where Mickey's boot had caught them, but my legs seemed to be working.

By the time I was in a position to follow him, Mickey was gone, and the hoplites were kicking open doors and shouting orders. I didn't fancy getting a beating from the law as well, so I scarpered out a side door when the hoplites came in the front. There was the stench of smoke in the air – someone had probably dropped a match into all that barley.

Mickey Finn was likely hoping that he could escape in the confusion, but I knew where he was going. I checked the prophecy again, "Honour the Carneia". Good choice.

The Carneia field was already packed with revellers, half of whom were wearing masks, and half of whom were covered in flowers. Cephorites, precariously balanced on top of ten foot stilts, picked their way through the crowds, dangling copper censers between their legs. Flocks of market kids chased after them, daring each other to grab the censers or climb the stilts.

I made my way to the lane that ran from the back of the temple towards the field. There were blood drops on the stones, and I reckoned I'd probably hit Mickey in the leg with that wild shot. I didn't have the gun, but I went after him anyway. I knew that I was looking for a limping man, and I knew that he'd be going to 'honour the gods'.

The far side of the Carneia field was dominated by an effigy of Demeter thirty feet tall, made of pine wood and barley straw. At the end of the festival it would be burnt to the ground. Four kaleidoscope lanterns had been placed around the effigy on rotating clockwork posts. They made an awful noise as they turned, and filled the air with multi-coloured light beams, so of course there was a jostling knot of people gathered to watch them. When I bent down to peer between their legs I could see Mickey on his knees at the front, placing an offering at Demeter's feet.

"Mickey!"

I'd had enough running and fighting by that point, so I hoped Mickey would feel the same.

Naturally, he ran for it.

The crowd was a nearly solid wall on every side, so he took the only direction still open and climbed, heading straight up the side of the effigy. I'm not sure what he thought he was going to accomplish, and I sure as hell wasn't going to go after him, but I shoved my way to the front and craned up at him. He was already ten foot above me by that point, and still dragging himself up the tightly packed straw bales. It occurred to me that he might be able to make some sort of jump from there into the crowd and give me the slip again, but the paper tape said 'Beware of heights'. I wasn't going anywhere.

Three Frog-heads in the crowd saw what was going to happen before I did. The effigy of Demeter was designed to be a bonfire, not a climbing tower. It wouldn't have held my weight, and it sure as hades didn't hold Mikey's. There was an almighty crack from somewhere inside the structure, and then it came down like a sack of onions, scattering straw, splinters, and festival goers in every direction. Naturally most of it fell right on top of Mickey Finn.

I stood there for a moment looking at Mickey's lifeless hand, which was sticking out from under the rubble. Figured he'd be dead after all that effort.

I took one last look at the Raven's prophecy. All true enough, but it hadn't helped me get my man, which was probably exactly what the Raven had intended. I chucked the paper on top of Mickey, and muttered 'Get stuffed' under my breath as I walked away. Next time I had a case, I'd go to the soothsaying rats over at the Arouraidrome and save myself the trouble.

Q

… is for **Quarry**

The Quarry

The quarry lurks on the edge of town, above the park, beyond a screen of trees.

You can see into it from the playground behind the nursery school, if you stand on tiptoes by the metal railings and squint through the trees. The little children are drawn to the fence by the sound of the quarry siren, which howls a warning before every blast.

"Underneath the rock it's full of tunnels," Will whispers excitably in Hazel's ear, "like a …" he struggles for the right image, "like a bath sponge!"

"How do you know?"

Will juts his chin in the air and answers with the all dignity a five year old can muster, "I just do."

The quarry siren gives a second blast, shutting them up for a moment. In the echoing silence afterwards she whispers back, "Who made the tunnels?"

Will puts on his dramatic voice, "Monsters!"

"Monsters?!"

"Yes, but you can't see them."

She makes a face. "If you can't see them how do you they are there?"

"You can't see them," he says, "but you can *feel* them. When you are looking right at them you tingle! And if they come close to you then you tingle more, and you mustn't move. If you move then they know you are there, and they will get you! They will drag you off into the tunnels and no one will ever see you again!"

Hazel is scared in spite of herself. "I don't believe you!" she says, but she does; and when the blast goes off a few minutes later, shaking the desks in the classroom they have been summoned back to, she stares out the window and thinks she feels a tingle — like a cold hand on her soul.

* * *

Five years later. Hazel is ten going on eleven, and the nursery school is a distant memory, but the quarry (disused now), is somewhere she unconsciously avoids.

The park below the old workings is a tangled mess of worn out paths and deadfall trees that the council hasn't gotten around to clearing out. In the bright sunlight of a drowsy summer, when autumn is an eternity away, it is a playground for Hazel and her friends. It's only ten minutes from home on foot, five on a bike. Provided they are back well before dark, when the park fills up with less savoury inhabitants, their parents don't mind them going.

Inevitably a gang has formed: Amanda, Louise, Tom, and James, with Hazel sort of tacked on the end. Amanda is the one in charge, a gregarious tomboy where Hazel is a loner on a hand-me-down bike. Most days Amanda chooses where they will go.

Today it's the far end of the park, where the unkempt tree line gives over to proper woods, which are even more unkempt. This is the side furthest from the town, and it has hills and old quarry works all behind it, which are too dangerous for children to play in. Naturally this means children are drawn there as surely as if the quarry siren was still sounding.

Amanda is sweet on Tom, which means she wants to do stupid, daring, things to impress him, which he probably doesn't notice — like drag them all up a steep path, so overgrown that James has to jump up and down on some of the plants to get them out of the way.

Hazel doesn't like it. The path is so close and dark that it blocks out the summer heat entirely, and she's shivering. For no reason at all she's frightened; terrified. Something has its fingers in her guts, an unpleasant tingle.

"Amanda," she calls, "where does this go?"

Amanda pauses ten feet further up, one foot balanced on a root that crosses the path. "To the quarry."

"We aren't supposed to go there."

This is the wrong thing to say, and she knows it right away from the looks the others give her. You are not supposed to be frightened of anything other than the bootleg horror movies James gets from his brother.

"Oh come on. It's just the quarry. It's full of water, we can swim in it. Or throw rocks in the water, or something."

Hazel wants to go with them, almost as much as she doesn't. She wants to fit in with the others. She's tired of being the strange one who gets left out, so she trails along behind them for a little while longer, through the dark tunnel of leaves, up the hill; but she gets further and further behind the others as time goes on. Amanda and Louise have vanished; Tom and James are just shadows on the path ahead, when something stops her.

It's as if someone brushed by her in the gloom, but no one's there. Her skin is tingling, or is it her gut? She tries to make her legs move, but they won't. Then suddenly she's crashing her way out of the woods, back towards the sunlight and the bikes.

Later she learns that the others went all the way to the quarry, and found a naked man sunbathing amongst the rubbish and the quarry spoil. All four of them ran away giggling, while the man tried desperately to put his clothes back on without exposing anything he shouldn't.

When Hazel's Mum hears about the naked man she forbids her to go anywhere near the quarry; which is a relief.

Now she doesn't have to tell anyone about the things she felt in the gloomy pathway.

* * *

Five more years. Now it's a bleak October evening, cold and damp. The sky over the town is sulphurous from reflected street lighting, but the actual streets are inky black, lined with blank-eyed terrace houses.

Hazel hurries furiously up the road, hands plunged deep into the pockets of her leather coat, eyes full of tears. How dare James speak to her that way! She feels like she was ten again, left behind by the others – humiliated. After she'd tried so hard to fit in. Well screw them!

She glances at the rain heavy clouds, feels the first spits of rain against her upturned face, and cuts left through the park gates. If she hurries, the shortcut might get her home before the rain hits in earnest.

She hasn't gone far before she realises that she has made a terrible mistake.

She isn't alone. There's a man behind her on the path, walking too quickly with his hood up. When she turns left onto the side path that leads to her street, he turns too, his sneakered feet slapping on the tarmac. She feels a sick, tense, panic. She's seen a dozen film's that start just like this, and she knows how they end. The park has a reputation – not a place a girl should go after dark. Why didn't she go the long way round? Why didn't she stay with her friends?

"James?" she calls out, trying to be brave, "is that you? Quit fooling around!"

The faceless man keeps coming. She can hear his breathing.

Hazel turns and runs, trying to lose him, but somehow he keeps pace, then gets ahead of her. She can see the streetlights of her road, just beyond the hedge, but the man gets to the side gate first and she backs away from the safety of houses.

She scrambles up the grass bank to the top path; loses a shoe; skids on the gravel; tries to reach a gate, a streetlight, any sort of safety; but she can't get away from him. In desperation she plunges into the bushes. She's gotten so turned around that she doesn't even know where she is, but there are trees ahead and she might be able to lose him.

There is darkness, rain, trees that loom out of the shadows as she scrambles up a slope she can't even see.

Hazel blunders out of the tree line onto a bald expanse of rubble and patchy grass. Twenty feet in front of her the ground drops off an edge, and she can just about make out an expanse of black water at the bottom. It takes her a moment to realise where she is – after all she's never seen it – and an old fear rushes to join the new one. She's on the edge of the quarry, of course, staring down at the lake that's filled up the pit.

Somewhere in the trees, a branch cracks. She knows that the man is probably only half a minute behind her, and that he will be excited from the chase. She should start running again, but she doesn't.

Instead she stares at the dark water and feels something – a creeping, tingling, sensation; as if cold water is trickling down her spine. Even though she can see that there is nothing there except old stones and water, she feels that there is. She feels as if something – no, many things – are creeping over the bare rocks toward her: watching her with invisible eyes, whispering with inaudible voices, touching her with intangible hands.

The man has left the wood. Hazel can see him out of the corner of her eye, approaching across the open ground. He probably thinks she is frozen in terror at the sight of him, but she is remembering little Will whispering in her ear 'If you move then they will get you!'

She risks a glance at the approaching man. His hood has

slipped back on his head and she can see his face, it is grey and yellow in the grey and yellow light. His mouth is open, and his eyes are wild. Can he feel the tingling? Of course not! It's just a stupid story from when she was a baby! She has to run! fight! scream! something; but she stands still, not daring to move.

The sensation is getting stronger. Now it feels like lightning is about to strike. Every hair on her body is standing on end. Even the rain has been banished, driven away by the static charge in the air. She feels that a million unseen creatures are pressing in on every side of her.

The man steps forward and reaches out. He's about to grab her, but something stops him short. He looks around, and his eyes grow wide, as if he can see something that she can't. He snaps his hand back, shakes his head. Then he starts to slap at his own body, smacking at his jacket with frenzied movements.

Hazel doesn't move, even as the man goes wild five inches away. She doesn't turn her head, or pull away. Only her eyes are alive, so she only half sees what happens next.

There is a ripping noise. It might be grass uprooting, or some piece of buried garbage catching on a shoe, but it sounds like cloth being torn apart by a hundred claws. There is a wind, and the wind is full of claws. The man cries out in pain. She hears him swear, "What the hell!" and then everything goes silent. Slowly the sense of presence draws away. The tingling fades. The cold October rain begins to fall again. When she finally dares to look around again there is no sign of the man.

Later, when Hazel tells her story to the Police, she says that she thinks he must have fallen into the quarry pond. The pond is so deep and treacherous that no one expects to be able to find his body, so after a dozen sympathetic questions they let her go.

When she gets outside she glances up at the hills beyond

the town, where the quarry lurks in the gloom behind the leafless trees, and feels a tingle deep inside; but she turns her back and hurries away home.

R

… is for **Rain**

Rain City

I am watching the rain run down the window. I am sick, and have been sicker. I am supposed to be recovering. My mind is ready to move again but my body will not oblige.

It is all I can do to drag my chair to the window and stare at the rain. Heavy drops are plummeting out of the grey sky and planting themselves on the other side of the glass, vibrating in the updraft.

Pinioned against the glass the drops succumb to gravity. They jerk this way and that – sometimes sideways, sometimes downwards – until they converge on certain well worn highways; express routes towards the bottom of the window.

On their way down the glass the raindrops meet rivals and start to race. They veer towards one another. They collide, merge, devour. Small raindrops vanish into the bodies of large ones and cease to exist. My exhausted heart starts to race. I am imagining the same process happening inside me, one set of tiny cells devouring another. I do not know which side is winning.

A new raindrop catches my eye. It is high up, just starting its journey. It moves erratically, seeming to defy gravity. Only my eyes are moving, following it. Another drop approaches and my chosen droplet devours it. It grows bigger and jerks downwards, leaving a snail trail of water behind it. It is closer now.

I think that I can see movement inside the drop – whirling particles of pale grey. Maybe these specks are actually inside my eye, but no, I decide that they are real. When the drop touches another, the specks surge across first, bridging the gap. This is not just an absorption but an invasion. The specks are making an attack. They overwhelm all resistance before dragging the new territory into their own.

The droplet is growing closer, approaching head height. I let my head sink forward until my forehead is resting on he glass. It is cold. The raindrop fills my vision.

Inside the raindrop there is structure. I can see buildings, towns, cities. I am seeing them magnified by the curve of the water so that they appear distorted and fantastical. When another water drop runs into first the structures are cast down and then built up again. I imagine a series of calamities. After each collision countless millions of these tiny creatures are exterminated, only to build again. The microscopic towers are re-erected; strategies for military defence are conceived and enacted; tiny politicians declare that this new age will be the finest yet, while minuscule prophets predict its doom. I am seeing all this happen in montage time while the raindrop advances towards its next collision. Do my own cells do the same? Do they regroup after each viral assault to rebuild – what? The same me as before the illness or something different?

The raindrop is heading straight towards the largest drop yet, an actual puddle of vertical water that will absorb it and wash it away. At the last moment it veers away intact.

It is a golden age inside the drop. New structures are unfolding before my eyes. Tiny explorers are launching outwards to found droplets of their own. This is civilisation, exploration. The same processes built my cells over geological ages, and they are just as fragile.

Now the raindrop is plummeting. It is on its final sprint towards the bottom of the window, where the droplets merge together into one vibrating sea. The city inside the drop is at the height of its civilisation. Its spires are soaring rotifer constructions. Its people must have art, beauty, culture, hopes, dreams. When they reach the bottom will they survive? or will they simply dissolve and be no more?

I am too tired to follow it further. I am unable to predict their fate, as I am unable to predict my own. I will just have to trust the stubbornness of those unseen builders, and their will to survive.

I close my eyes.

S

… is for **Statue**

The Figurine

Mr Norris would soon come to regret buying the figurine from the car boot sale.

It was a lively caricature of a man, made of dark wood, with ivory eyes and ivory teeth, and a walking stick made of a porcupine quill. It was not the sort of object that Mr Norris would normally have bought for himself, but something about the touch-polished ebony caught his attention. He had the odd feeling that the blank white eyes were actually watching him, and although the effect was slightly disturbing it was also fascinating.

When he looked up from examining the figure he saw that the seller, a middle-aged man with slightly narrowed eyes, was watching him keenly.

"Expensive, I suppose?" Mr Norris asked casually.

"No no, not at all. Just a pound, thanks."

Mr Norris turned the figurine over suspiciously. At that price he thought that it must be a mass-produced knick-knack, but it showed every sign of being handcrafted.

"Just an old thing of my wife's," the man said quickly.

Mr Norris handed over his money before the seller changed his mind, tucked it into his bag, and walked away without noticing the strange – almost pitying – look that the seller directed at his back.

He placed the figurine on a shelf in the bedroom, with its back against a line of rarely used books, and thought no more about it.

A few days later Mr Norris suffered a horrible dream. Someone was bending over him as he slept. A pair of burning luminous eyes were staring into his own. He was pinned in place by them. He awoke covered in sweat, feeling as if he had been nailed to his bed. But it was only a dream after all, and he rolled over and tried to forget it.

The dream came back, however, night after night, and each time it was worse. He felt that he had been paralysed, or perhaps transformed into stone or lead, while this awful figure thrust its bony fingers into his open mouth and tried to crawl its way inside. He woke pale and aching, convinced that things were being removed from him bit by bit each time he slept. The dream was so awful that he remained upset the whole day; unwell at work, and morose at home.

After the fifth repetition of the dream Mr Norris began to believe that the figurine was somehow involved in his nightmares, although its ivory smile was as cheerful as ever. He turned it to face the wall, and when that didn't seem to be enough to him, shoved it into his sock drawer.

That night he slept easily for the first time in a week, but in the middle of the night there came a scratching and a rustling that almost woke him. He rolled over and half opened his eyes, and saw a white ivory glare staring back!

He opened his mouth to scream; a mistake. Dark wooden fingers seized his tongue in a vice-like grip and pulled, making way for the thin arm to thrust its way down his throat. Mercifully he lost consciousness before the shape began to climb inside.

When Mr Norris woke for a second time he thought that the dream had returned, for he felt paralysed by fear, but then he realised that it wasn't fear that rooted him to the spot, it was the little nails that attached his feet to his wooden plinth – he was now the statue!

He screamed but made a sound; thrashed his limbs without stirring; glanced frantically around without moving his eyes — there was no motion to be had because he was trapped inside the figurine! He beat against the wooden confines from within, like a man trapped within a coffin, but nothing happened. For an unknown time he was lost to panic, unable to comprehend what had happened to him.

He was returned to his senses by a single question that cut through the terror — if he was now trapped in the figurine, what had become of the thing that had been there before?

The sun rose, the alarm rang, and something wearing Mr Norris' body climbed out of the bed, said good morning to his wife, and glanced at Mr Norris where he sat on the shelf before leaving the room.

That evening the creature in Mr Norris' body came into the bedroom alone and walked over to the shelf; where he stood in silence, staring at Mr Norris, while Mr Norris stared back in impotent fury.

"I know how you feel." The creature almost had Mr Norris' voice down pat, but Mr Norris could tell the difference.

"That was me once." The creature reached a hand out towards the statue, and then apparently thought better of it and pulled back.

"I'm afraid there is no way to get your own body back, so you might as well stop worrying about it," the double said. "Believe me, I tried. Tried everything."

Mr Norris raged. He yelled back at him in his mind. He clawed his unmoving fingers and tried to sink them into his stolen flesh. The false Mr Norris continued on regardless.

"But, there is a way. You can take someone else. You can't have this body any more, it's mine. But you can have another body." The creature gave a short sour laugh. "You won't believe me. I didn't when it was me, but you will."

"Never!" Mr Norris shouted, but the creature was already gone.

For the next few days Mr Norris was forced to watch his double live his life. At first he spent the time locked up in inner misery, refusing to accept what had happened. He hoped to go mad, because if he was mad he wouldn't have to experience what was happening. But, slowly, he came to his senses and realised that he still had a chance. Whatever had been inside the statue had stolen his body — now he had to work out how to steal it back.

He refused to believe what the creature had told him. The creature had terrorised him at night, therefore it must be possible for him to animate the statue too. Having realised this, Mr Norris set his mind to discovering the secret — after all he had nothing but time.

Moving the figurine's body turned out to be impossible, but through sheer determination he discovered that he could force his consciousness (if that is what it was), outside his wooden prison. He could move around the room, maybe as far as twenty feet before he was brought up short. More than enough to reach his body in the bed, but here he was out of luck. No matter what he tried he could not affect his peacefully sleeping body. It felt like the flesh body was the one made of wood, while Mr Norris was made of something more flimsy than smoke.

He could take his wife's body, but that was a horrible thought, and didn't get him any closer to recovering his own body. Even if he was willing to take someone else's body — and the truth was that the idea was starting to grow on him — no one else was going to sleep close enough to the figurine for him to get inside.

Or were they?

One week after losing his body Mr Norris found himself taken off the shelf by his own stolen hands. Once again his doppelgänger spoke to him, and this time his voice was comfortable, at home in the body he had taken.

"Okay in there mate? Yeah, I bet you aren't. Remember,

I've been where you were. And look, I'm sorry I took your body, but what was I supposed to do?" Mr Norris saw an unfamiliar look of distress cross his pilfered face.

"I was in there for so long. I had my chance and I took it. It wasn't pretty." He held the figure up for a moment and then placed it in a cardboard box, a cardboard box full of ornaments and junk. "Now it's your turn."

Of course, Mr Norris realised, it was back to the car-boot sale for him. Back to the car-boot, where someone would buy him, someone with a body he could steal, and the whole cycle would start all over again.

He couldn't wait.

T

… is for **Tsunami**

Persistence of Memory

Jeannie, oh Jeannie, where are you!

The water splashes softly at the sides of my boat. Overhead the seagulls wheel and scream, but they have no answer for me.

I put my oars back in the water and pull. I am already damp with salt water and sweat, but I bend my back and row on, picking my way down the flooded streets. The water is dark with suspended silt – as if there are clouds drifting beneath the keel of my boat. When the clouds part I can see the tops of cars, the lids of litter bins and post boxes, the remains of the city, passing beneath me.

"Jeannie!" I shout it again and again, stupidly, until my throat is sore.

I rest again till the madness passes, and my voice recovers, looking around me at the empty houses. The windows on the second floors are broken where the water has rushed into them, and I catch glimpses of furniture floating on the water inside. Here, a waterlogged mattress has fetched up against an empty window frame, and there, I can see a room thick with drifting lampshades.

I try to place myself in the city, but all the landmarks have vanished or changed. Maps, memories, names, places; all are equally useless. I've been hauling myself along these sunken streets for days, sleeping in the boat, or on the occasional flat roof. The food I stuffed under my seat is damp and running out. My maps are useless. I'm starting to think that the city shifts around while I doze. I'm afraid that I will wake up one morning to find that everything has become the open sea, and that I will be adrift forever.

Not yet, Jeannie, not yet.

I scull to the corner of the street and try my best to make out the name bolted to the wall under the waterline, but there is too much detritus in the way. I once tried diving to find a street name to place on my map, but the water was full of tangling debris that nearly dragged me down – too dangerous to try that again!

The houses I rowed past today were unfamiliar, but from the end of the street I can see a church spire emerging from the water in the middle distance, and I think that perhaps I recognise it.

The afternoon sun beats down on my back as I row. It is blazing out of a clear sky, scattering brilliant sparkles across the floodwater. I have to squint to see at all, and this transforms the pinpoints into clouds of dancing stars. I remember lying on a beach once, long ago, looking at the sea, and thinking those stars were beautiful, but here they fill me with dread. It's like the city is dissolving.

Oh Jeannie, where are you?

A mat of flotsam has fetched up against the submerged roof of the church. Tree branches are tangled up with bicycles, and sandwich boards, and packing crates, and plastic bags – which trail in the current like jellyfish tendrils. Snarls of willow-herb and salt-rush cling to the rubbish. They are turning the spire into an island; perhaps this new land will spread like a skin until all the forgotten things are hidden underneath it.

Seabirds and pigeons jostle together on the narrow ledges of the spire – the stone angels are stained white with their droppings. When I draw closer, after two hours of steady rowing, I am sure that it is the steeple of St. John's.

I thrust the oars into the bottom of the boat, and balance on the thwarts to scan the floodwaters around me. Over to the left is a submerged house with a distinctive white roof – surely this must be Ivy Street, and the buildings beyond it Oak Street. I twist around in excitement, and for a moment the city jumps into focus; landmarks emerge from the concealing waters. Yes! That tall window marks the back of the bank that lay on the corner. And there, that expanse of water must be the park! Even as I see it, the view starts to drift apart again, but I'm certain I am right. I'm close!

I drop down to the bench and heave on the oars, hauling the boat up the street. The seagulls screech at my departing back, happy to see me go.

At the end of the street a mass of tangled metal juts clear of the water. A truss of dark grey beams has been twisted like a corkscrew and then folded almost in half on itself. With a gut wrenching start I realise that it is the footbridge that crosses the train tracks at the bottom of our road.

The recognition brings with it a flood of terrifying images. Suddenly I'm back in the darkness, scrambling to stuff myself into the neighbour's car as the water comes rushing up the street. It pours around the wheels of the car, gurgling out of the drains, rising so fast. A wave of it comes washing down the road, a foot high, overflowing the curbs; then another. The night is full of the blare of horns and the scream of metal – maybe I heard the footbridge collapsing.

After that I recall only montage flashes: the howl of the evacuation sirens; blue lights flashing in the darkness; my friends holding me back when I realise Jeannie isn't there; the wailing of babies in the shelter; my own frantic tears. Then a long blankness before I wind up here, with a rickety boat and a pair of oars. Oh Jeannie! Never mind. I'm here now.

I wait until the memories slip back under the water. There are no more waves, no more sirens, it was all long ago. The flood has claimed this place, and it appears that it will never leave.

I nose the boat into what remains of Oak Street, and am finally surrounded by familiar things. Half my life rises from the concealing waters — the places where Jeannie and I met, loved, made a home. Here is the bed and breakfast on the corner, there the rotted curtains of our neighbours' windows, and then, finally, our home.

The upstairs of the house is knee deep in water, and dark. The sun is setting, and I'm glad, because it means I don't have to see the damage that the water has done.

Something splashes in the corner of the room as I clamber through the window; I think it might be a rat, but I can't see it. A pale mass of bare mattress glimmers just under the water's surface — I'm in the spare bedroom. The door that leads to the hallway has been pushed open by the water.

"Jeannie," I whisper hoarsely, "I'm coming."

I forge on through the flooded house, throwing my body against the sodden weight of closed doors. The stairway is a bottomless well. A scum of once-precious objects clogs the surface of the water, drifting away as I wade through them. I hardly recognise the place. It has been transformed into something rich and strange, as the poem says.

One last heave against a heavy door and I have reached our bedroom. The last rays of the sun angle through the window, illuminating what is left of the bed I left unmade that fateful night. The mattress has come away from the bedstead and the wardrobes have floated open, but the dresser stands clear of the water.

With trembling hands I reach for the picture frame that leans against the wall on top of the dresser. Somehow it has remained untouched, as I knew it would.

Jeannie, oh my Jeannie. I trace your face under the glass with my fingertips; I'd almost forgotten what you looked like.

When I return to the boat I wrap the picture carefully in cloth and hold it to my breast like a lifeline. The current plucks at the bows and the boat turns, picking up speed as the water draws it away from the last familiar things.

I let myself drift; I have what I came for.

U

… is for **Universe**

Vanishing World

Notes found in a pocketbook dropped at the back of Waverley Station

I can't actually remember where I was when I first heard the news.

It seems silly doesn't it, not to remember something as important as the end of the world, but back then it all seemed so abstract, a scientific curiosity and nothing more. That's probably the way with all truly important things – you don't understand just how important they are till afterwards, when it's already too late.

In Parliament I heard they called it a 'superimposition', or some such scientific word. The papers were more sensational, they called it a collision. Professor James Minwell, the famous polymath, had announced his discovery in The New Scotsman – our world was crashing headlong into another one. Some other version of our stars, of New Scotland, of Edwinsburgh, was set to sweep through the world, like two waves passing through each other. The science minister came on the Radiogram to tell us that there was nothing to fear; we would be lucky to see anything of this great conjunction other than through a telescope's lens, certainly nothing for the common man or boy to worry themselves about.

The observatory duly put a view through its 'scope on sale for a penny a shot, and I could see the back end of the queue from my shoeshine spot by the station door. No doubt someone was alarmed by the news, but I was pleased by a steady stream of customers wanting their shoes perfect before they took their turn at the telescope.

All of that changed soon enough, when the disappearances began. It was the little things that went first, odds and ends, stray cats and lost dogs, unattended bags on the station platforms, and narrow lanes where no one lived; but the bigger things came after.

I remember looking up when the men ran past, yelling that King's Street had been swept away. Dumbly I thought they were speaking of some sort of landslide, a flood, or a coal gas explosion, but it was that other world of course. The whole street had simply vanished, leaving nothing behind but mis-connected tram tracks and alleys that went nowhere. There wasn't even a gap or a ruin, just nothing. By the time the stars had begun to wink out in the sky the truth was clear, ours was the weaker world, and like the tracks left by feet in the sand all trace of it would be washed away as that tide came in.

I was just one face in the crowd when it gathered back at the observatory doors to demand that the great men come out to answer the shouted questions. The chief astronomer alone ventured to poke a pale face above the balcony rail and brave the yells and random missiles. The mood was very angry. If I understood him right — over the jeers and cries — there was but one hope, some scientific venture that the finest minds of New Scotland were attempting. Otherwise this foreign world would roll serenely onwards, undisturbed by our own more fragile reality, till nothing was left but scraps and traces.

That was when I really understood that this was no ephemeral crisis like the war in the Balkans or the wreck of the St. George, but the total extinction of everything we knew. The crowd knew it too. Some few continued to rage and rail against their fates, and others put their trust at once in Minwell's genius, but the rest went silently away, seeking only the comfort of their home fires – while they still had them.

Like many people I spent the following days in a daze. It was hard to take in what was happening, even when I could see the evidence in front of me. One day you could see the fluttering sails of the boats on the river, the next all the water was gone. One night I trudged home past the glitter of the Royal Post Office dome at the head of the Walk, the next morning the entire building had vanished. Even the stars could not keep their positions in the sky.

When the day of the experiment came I stayed at home, glued to the Radiogram. The SBC reporter was breathless as he described the arcing lightning of Minwell's Great Machine, which had been laid out along the river plain at Cambuslang. I could hear the crackle of the coils over the reporter's voice as they counted down to the crucial moment, just as I could hear the terrible roar of the explosion that destroyed the machine. The experiment had failed.

That was the end of it. One by one the voices on the Radiogram fell silent: the swaggering generals, the cajoling politicians, the begging priests. Only the bravest, or the most foolish, clung to the belief that something could still be done.

When disaster looms you find hope in the strangest of places. I can't remember who was the first to tell me that – just like the ocean and the beach – some of the things we left behind might, just might, get swept along with the tide and make it to the other side. Maybe it was the old man with the white spats who used to stop by each day, or maybe it was the wild eyed poet who begged for coins, before he too was no more. It's the smallest of things. No hope for any of us, but the thought that some signs of our works might poke through the smooth new sand and make someone stop to wonder where they came from. Maybe the Post Office dome has fetched up on a rooftop over in the other world already, perhaps the words the poet scrawled on the station wall are scribbled in some other city instead.

These were the thoughts that lay heavy on my mind that last day. Most of the city had already vanished, and those of us who were left followed the mundane rituals of our old lives for want of anything better to do. The man who put his foot on my shoeshine block probably had no more reason to be there that day than I did, but he'd put on his best shoes and best suit regardless, just as I had. I think he said hello, but I couldn't bear to meet his eyes.

Instead I bent to my work, pulling out polish and brush and cloth. No sooner had I put my brush to the leather, than I realised that the man inside the shoe was gone, washed away like everything else. Would I be next, or would the street, and the trains, and the tracks, and the bridge go first, leaving me on an empty earth, the last to vanish?

That was when I realised that I could keep on staring at the ground till the ground was gone, or go and look upon Edwinsburgh one last time while it was still there. I started to pack up my stuff, but I realised that I had no use for them either. Instead I left it there: shoe, polish, cloth, even this pocket book which perhaps, just perhaps, you are reading.

Most likely they will be erased from existence as soon as my back is turned, but I hold a little hope that they will somehow slip through the cracks into the new world to come and that someone will see them, and wonder, and remember us.

V

... is for Vegetation

The Green

We greet every morning the same, with napalm and herbicides.

At dawn the firemen head out to fight the advancing thorns of last night's growth; by noon they trudge home across the burn-back, soot black and exhausted. Children and old men – faces covered to keep out seeds and spores – hunt through the ash for the slightest specks of green that escape the flames, attacking them with knives; trowels; sticks. The children laugh; the old men scratch at skin turned green by mould and algae.

Normally I'd be amongst them.

Despite the efforts of the firemen and the weed hunters it is all we can do to keep one little area clear – Klay, the last city, our refugee camp. The rest of the world has long ago been lost to the green – turned into continents of thorn woods; savannahs of toxic blossoms; mountain ranges of strangling vines. Our war is no more than a desperate holding action.

I call Klay a city, because that is what my fellow Gardeners have always called it. Klay, the refuge; Klay, the surviving; Klay, white from ash and black from char. Really it is little more than a shanty town, clinging to the fringes of the real city of the same name, which was abandoned to the green long ago.

On one side the burn-back – an arc of incinerated soil bounded by cliff faces of leaves and branches. Then the clusters of tents and shacks, the narrow alleys with floors of corrugated plastic, the dung burners and herbicide sprays. In one doorway a pair of frightened eyes blink behind the cracked lenses of a gas mask, in the next an old woman worries at the purple stain of lichen papering her arm. Food packs change hands, babies scream, engines chug, mothers scrub their children raw to scrape off the algae; everything is tired. Everything is ugly.

Beyond the claustrophobic streets, the Gardeners' citadel. Ironically it used to be a botanical research station. The yellowed plastic facets of its geodesic dome have been patched with rusting steel since the Gardeners moved in. Normally I'd be up there straight after the burning, to argue and experiment in the dirty orange light of the Underdome; but Borok Singh, the High Reaper, has declared my experiments anathema, and I'm not there either.

At the back of the citadel the food factories crowd close, grinding oil seeps and bodies into nutrition paste. We are eating ourselves to stay alive, and the Gardeners tell us it's enough.

Finally, beyond even the food factories, an arc of wall 30 feet tall. White, towering, fractal veined by vines and poison blooms — the edge of the real Klay.

That's where I am, beyond the wall, beyond Klay.

Venturing into the green is forbidden, of course, but it's a token prohibition because no one in their right mind would want to do it. I wouldn't, if I had a choice. I'm a dead man walking. I'm still breathing, but that won't last. Even if I can dodge the hook thorns, and the venom blossoms, and the strangling vines; the green will still get under my skin. If I breathe, spores will burrow into my lungs. If I cut my skin, algae will infest my blood. If I somehow make it more than three days without dying first, then the creeping mosses will eat me from the outside—in.

I've protected myself as well as I can, of course, because I have a mission to complete. I've wrapped myself in plastic sheeting and soaked my skin with pesticides until it's gone as brown as the tree trunks I'm pushing past, wych elm and gall oak.

It's strangely quiet out here. Silence is something I'm no longer used to. Klay is five hundred thousand men and women crammed into an ever-shrinking noose of greenery; it is never silent. Here, though, there are only plants, and the green shrouded remains of the original Klay.

It is almost beautiful. In Klay we keep our eyes on the ground, and on each other. Green is the colour of death, and no one wants to look up at the advancing wall of plants encircling us, except through the distorting wash of a flamethrower. When we do, we see thorns and suckers, blind roots and stinging hairs, crawling moulds and rotten fecundity. Out here the green seems gentler. Nodding blossoms line trails of sighing grass and pungent herbs. Fields of flowers: white, blue, red, and purple, turn their faces upwards towards the sun. So what if their roots are planted on the skulls of men and the bones of women? I've only gone a mile and already the green has forgotten us.

I end the first day in the shelter of a concrete block that probably used to be the base of some soaring building. Thick cables of vine explode from its top like worms from a corpse, but there is a clear area of rubble at the base where I can spread my sterilised tarpaulin and try to rest.

I feel almost naked here, I'm so exposed. In Klay we smother ourselves in plastics and metals, ceramics and chemicals. We touch the world, when we must, through layers of rubber and vinyl. We breathe through filters and scrubbers. In the citadel, where the Gardeners concoct herbicides and bio-agents, sterilisation is a cultish obsession. The route to Borok Singh's Underdome is lined with gusting pressure curtains and decontamination sprays. But out here, the green is only millimetres away. I could reach out and touch it; it could reach down and touch me.

In the morning a tracery of shoots has descended from the

upper reaches of the block to enclose me, but I cut myself free with my machete and get back on the road. The other Gardeners will have missed me by now, but I don't think they will follow.

I gulp down three red squares from my food pack when the sun reaches its zenith. In the distance I can see my goal, three tree cloaked towers, massive enough to rise above the green. I've been travelling all day, but I don't think I'll reach them before nightfall. It is hard going, and it's a long way – which is the real key to why I'm here.

Everyone in our Klay knows that the ruined Klay was huge, but only I know the truth – this was once the capital of all humanity. When we spread out to the corners of the world, we did it from Klay. When we raised our grand towers across the globe, we raised them here first. And, of course, when we destroyed ourselves, we started here.

Borok Singh and the others don't even suspect. As far as they know, Klay is just a place we ended up – a patch of earth where we can make a last stand against what's chasing us. Only I understand that we've come full circle. Somewhere in those three towers is the heart, the root, the first seed, the place where the green was born.

The Gardeners see the green as an enemy, a vile thing, an evil force, so they make weapons to fight it. Marmorek Zuza extracts volatile oils to fuel our flamethrowers. Kaneeka Khal brews plagues from dead flesh to blight the air. Indra Holtz carves shears and machete blades from the plastic debris of the citadel's dome. Borok Singh, of course, turns children into soldiers and the rest of us into lab rats. Only I saw that the green was not a sickness, but simply sick. Not something to be fought, but something to be cured.

We used to live in harmony with plants, did you know that? Before the plague a gardener was someone who tended plants, not someone who fought them. I'm sure Borok Singh has forgotten that!

I didn't.

It seemed to me that something must have changed. An accident, an experiment. I didn't know what – I still don't – but the citadel's ancient records told me how and where, right here in Klay. I studied them for weeks, in secret, till I understood that, just possibly, I could undo what had happened if I could reach them place where the green began. That was when I decided I would create a cure instead of another weapon.

I have it here in my hand, Borok Singh's anathema. A simple tube of copper and vinyl, a year's labour – a recipe to undo what was done. All I have to do is reach the three towers before the green kills me.

I expected opposition. I thought I'd be fighting for my life. I equipped myself with one of Zuza's flamethrowers and a tank of napalm to go along with my plastic blade, but the green doesn't seem to be interested in me. I expected throttling lianas, venom roses, necrotising orchids. Instead – as the second day draws to a close – I find myself surrounded by purple flowers the size of ration plates. As the sun dips behind the distant trees, the flowers fold in upon themselves like closing fists, and new flowers, smaller and whiter, open underneath them.

I stop, fascinated. By rights these night blossoms should no longer exist. What's the point in opening flowers for insects that no longer live? But even as I think the thought a grey moth flutters across my path. It settles on an open flower, and I expect it to die, but a moment later it continues on its way.

Slow acting poison? It's possible, but the moth should have been dead long ago. It's accepted wisdom in Klay that the green has killed everything but us. The thought that something else still lives shocks me to the core. I'm so certain that I must have hallucinated the moth that I practically stumble into the flowers myself, but the air is full of moths by then, and I have to acknowledge the truth – it is only us that the green has killed.

Mechanically, I make camp in the shadows of an open tunnel, where bare stone keeps the plants at bay. The air is full of moths and the invisible whirr of bats. Bats! I've not seen another mammal since I was a child. In Klay, our Klay, any life that comes within reach of the green is killed in a hundred ways.

But not here.

How? Why? The old records – they talk of plant science, genetic manipulation, strain grafting. The cure in my pocket implies a disease of human making. The scattered pieces of knowledge, everything I've painfully uncovered, come together in a flash. I imagine the scientists of old Klay – men like Borok Singh and Indra Holtz – brewing up a weapon. How clever they must have thought themselves, working out a way to turn the very plants on their enemies, programming them to kill. Madmen! Monsters! We killed ourselves!

The realisation is enough to stun me. All along I thought that I was following in the footsteps of people like myself, desperate scientists searching for a cure before the Green overwhelmed them; instead I was recapitulating the work of murderers.

My food pack lies forgotten at my side. My eyes are fixed on the bare stone of the tunnel mouth, but my mind is elsewhere. All that death. All those years of panicked retreat, of plant infested bodies, of loved ones left behind. We did it to ourselves!

For a long time, I barely move.

The moon rises over the distant towers like a flower blooming. I should be sleeping, but instead I lie awake in the darkness of the tunnel watching it. Knowing the truth doesn't change my mission. There are still people back in Klay, fighting for their lives, and the cure in my pocket can save them. It shouldn't make any difference how the green came to be — but it does.

I drag myself out of the tunnel with the first glimmer of dawn, leaving my plastic sheet spread out behind me. I'm neglecting basic precautions now, but I don't care, my mind is on the goal ahead, and not what comes after.

I hike through the heat of the day, under a canopy of unbroken green. Trees are piled on top of trees here, jungle giants as tall as the Underdome, clinging to the skeletons of ancient skyscrapers. Strangle vines descend from their under-branches like lethargic serpents, their distal ends wrapped lazily around antique bones. They sway gently in the still air, and I give them a wide berth, but they are barely interested in me. The bones they are holding could be as old as the city itself. Even so, it's the first sign of hostile plant life I've seen since I lost sight of the city wall, and it brings back the old familiar fears. Nervously I check myself for barbs and thorns, moulds and lichen growths. The fingers of my left hand have a greenish tinge, when did that happen? In the murky sunlight my arm looks blotched with green too, but I can't tell for certain.

I swallow a handful of anti-algaics with a mouthful of tepid water from my flask and push on.

By noon, day three, I am in the shadows of the towers. This is the core of Klay that was. The buildings here are so huge that they have resisted the predations of the green; or rather the green has not touched them. There is open ground here. A lawn, such as I have read about of old. Manicured trees; ragged beds of flowers; neat paths.

It is a trap, of course. The trees are choke apples, the flowers are butcher's bloom, the lawn would probably fill me full of poison barbs before I'd gone five paces across it. One last joke by the men who created this place. Borok Singh would have loved them.

Luckily I have a lifetime's experience fighting the green. I fire up my flamethrower and move forwards, washing the deadly plants with fire till the air fills wish ash and I imagine a squadron of firemen at my side. When the flame is not enough I release Kaneeka Khal's finest herbicide gasses from a canister strapped to my back. The toxic cloud burns back the needle grass and rots the choke apples on the bough before they can open. When both are exhausted I have my blade and my polyvinyl armour.

Finally I'm inside, taking petal strewn steps two at a time before the green can regroup and find a way to come after me. The flamethrower is exhausted, the gas canister too, so I drop them and move on. The vial. The vial is all I need.

The walls of the tower are plastered with elegant script in languages I don't understand, and logos that I recognise from the Underdome archives. I've seen them stamped on rusting metal cabinets and ancient plastic file sheets. Here they are proudly displayed on wall plaques, and the rims of long dead video screens. The entrance steps open onto luxury waiting rooms stained grey and brown by old moulds. Beyond, in the central atrium, cryptic laboratories are visible behind crazed walls of glass. This is the place.

I consult a floor directory. The names of what must be defunct companies are unreadable, but the topmost floors are marked with the same logo from the Underdome. I have to go up.

The lifts are long dead, like everything else electrical, so I bang through the door into the vertiginous concrete of an emergency stairwell. The shaft is cold, tall, and choked with pendent seed pods the size of a child's closed fist.

I jerk back, covering my mouth by instinct, but it is already too late. The pods crackle open, showering me with luminous cyanotic seeds that swirl through the dead air of the stairwell. I slam back through the door, head down, but I can already feel my exposed flesh burning. Stupid! I should have known better!

I rip back the tattered plastic of my over-cloak and slather myself with tar-brown contraseptics, scrubbing my flesh raw to scrape off the seeds. It's no more than a delaying action. I estimate that I'll have an hour, maybe two, before the toxins have overcome my system — it will have to do.

I bind the burns with strips of pvc, wrapping them around my arms and hands like a boxer. I put more over my head, and across my face. It's stifling, but it's enough to brave the stairs a second time.

Leaves. Roots. Searing seeds — I struggle through them all, and emerge burnt and gasping on the 40th floor with the evening sun slanting through smoke brown windows.

The 40th floor is a lab — a single chamber mazed with lines of hydroponic tanks and glass fronted terrariums. Lines of testing benches, their tops littered with the rusting carcases of computers and analytical machines, surround the open centre of the room, where a single towering structure dominates — a planter ten meters across, inside which rests a monstrous bulb.

The bulb is four times my height. It is fecund, rotting, bursting with aberrant leguminous life. The mottled surface is studded with root nodules and saprophytic outgrowths. A mass of vines bursts from the upper part, twisting their way into the crumbling concrete structure of the building. Here and there, there are flowers, roots, buds, and blossoms.

I stumble at the sight of it, and have to cling to the workbenches to stay on my feet.

This is the green — the heart, the root, and seed of it. Scientists swarm, birthing it with gene splices and mutagens, their movements blurring like a haze of green corpusles. Each of them wears the Underdome's icon on their back, and Borok Singh's face on their head. But no, I'm hallucinating … I think. The poison is in my bloodstream; from the spore wash, or the algal growths, or the air itself, I can't tell any more.

I use the bench to push myself upright again and inch

forward. The cure is in my hand. The copper is cold against my palm. All I have to do is pop the top and drive it forward, the gas injector inside will do the rest. The bulb is the first step in the green's expansion, the only place where the ancient weaponised genome of Klay can be found intact. Once it combines with the virus suspension inside the copper vial it will become a plague to rival the green itself. Everything created here will wither, and burn, and die. I just need to take the final step.

Only … am I just another killer like the madmen that made this thing? Like Borok Singh and the other Gardeners? Outside the desperate burn-back of Klay I've seen beauty. Such a contrast with our squalid scrabbling. The green is no-longer the aberration, we are. We killed ourselves, over and over, in our arrogance. Why should we live?

My vision blurs again. The floor won't stay level under my feet. Is this the green, getting inside my head, or a real decision? I don't know. I do know that I've risked everything to come here. I have to go through with it!

But I remember the moths; the bats; the night flowers under the blossom moon. Life goes on. The green was designed to kill mankind alone — when it's done the world can rest; we can rest; I can rest.

The sun chooses that moment to set, spearing a last few rays of light through the broken windows. It reminds me of the napalm wash of home, and I let myself sink down against a wall until I'm sitting on the floor.

Pale green flowers open on the fecund hulk of the bulb, and I watch them. Moths flutter in through the empty window frames in search of pollen, and I watch them too. Outside the flower fields must be folding their petals shut, all around the world. Only in Klay, sad desperate Klay, is there pain and death.

Well, let them die.

W

... is for **Windblown**

The Traveller

Jeanie was jerked awake by a crash above her head. It sounded like a tree branch had fallen on the roof, but she knew it couldn't be that, no matter how fiercely the wind was howling through the eaves, because her room was right below the attics, six storeys up.

Rain was throwing itself at the windows in squalls, and she could hear it dripping on the ceiling above her head. She was certain that something had staved in the roof, so she wrapped herself in her thickest coat and scrambled up the attic steps to see what had happened.

In the cavern of the attic, rain was falling; the wind had peppered the roof with missing tiles. Jeanie stood with one hand clutching the steep ladder that led up to the roof, wondering what to do. The wind howled, flipping up the hatch at the top of the ladder, and she distinctly heard a voice cry "Help! Help!" from up above. Someone was up there! She had to help!

The hatch opened onto a flat crest of rooftop, crowded with chimney stacks and battered with rain. A forest of aerials thrummed and clanged in the wind. A man was tangled up in them, head down and heels up. He was dressed in a huge olive overcoat that flapped in the wind like a sail. He had a brown hat clamped to his head and a battered leather case clutched in his hands.

Jeanie was afraid that at any moment the wind would wrench the man free and hurl him off the edge of the roof, so she rushed to his aid, grabbing hold of his arms and bracing herself against the rough bricks of the nearest chimney. Aerials whipped at her, and cold pellets of rain battered her face, but somehow she was able to help him down, then lead him, arms locked over shoulders, into the shelter of the attic.

Drip, drip, went the man, as he stood shivering in the insulated gloom of her hallway. His overcoat was soaked through, and the pale face under the hat was plastered with strands of hair. Without thought she thrust a towel into his hands – he struggled to hold both it and the case – and pushed him through the bathroom door.

"Use the shower!" she insisted, pressing her face to the textured glass. A few moments later she heard the hiss of the water, and turned towards the kitchen. Only then did she realise that she was half undressed with a strange man in her house!

By the time the man emerged from the steam-wet bathroom, wrapped in Jeanie's terrycloth robe and holding a neatly folded pile of wet clothes in his hands, she was properly dressed. In the glow of the hallway light she could see that he was darkly handsome, with pale skin framed by black hair. His eyes were piercing blue, and honest, and when he said: "Thank you, thank you.", his voice was heavily accented.

Jeanie tried to offer him the hot mug of tea that she had made for him, but his hands were full with the clothing, so she led him to the kitchen and helped him hang them on the drying rack. When the huge brown coat was hung up, she saw that it had been ripped through in a dozen places by the sharp metal of the aerials.

Jeanie sat down at one end of the old wooden kitchen table, and the man sat at the other, resting his elbows awkwardly on the wood as he sipped the tea. The leather case was pressed between his feet, where it could not slip away.

What do you say to a stranger the wind dropped on your

roof? Jeanie had no idea. The stranger, for his part, could only explain that he was a traveller, trying to get home. She understood that there had been a war, or a job, she wasn't sure which, that had taken him far away. All he had was the coat on his back and his case.

What could she do except take him in? So she made him up a bed on the fold out cot in the living room, and retreated to her room.

The next day the traveller climbed back to the attic and set to work fixing the holes in the roof. The rain had blown away with the darkness and now the attic was filled with blustery sunlight. Jeanie watched him work from the stairs. He had rolled up his shirt-sleeves, and was manoeuvring the tiles into place above his head, so that the sunlight shining through the gaps in the roof highlighted the play of muscles on his arms. When she realised that she was staring she hurried down the stairs.

Back in the silence of the kitchen she ran her hands lightly along the stiff brim of the traveller's battered fedora, which was hanging from the edge of the drying rack. She looked at the coat too, seeing how big the tears were. When she stepped into the living room to open the curtains she saw that the traveller had left his case by the foot of the cot bed. It was made of scuffed brown leather, with a pair of handles and a brass clasp. The initials N.B. were faintly imprinted on the side.

Jeanie felt a sudden temptation to open it, and put a hand on the lock, but then she remembered how the traveller had clutched it to him as if it was the most important thing in the world, and felt ashamed.

Over the next few days the traveller seemed to settle into Jeanie's life, filling a gap she hadn't known was there. Always quiet, unassuming, looking at everything as if it was a mystery to him. He was good with his hands, able to fix a sticking door or a creaking floorboard with ease; but when it came to radios or telephones, light fittings or gas rings, books or steam kettles, he was at a loss. When he was done fixing things for the day, he would climb the ladder to the roof and watch the weather through the open hatch.

Jeanie found herself dreaming of a life with the traveller. She imagined showing him the city — introducing him to the park by the river, and the lions at the zoo. They could ride the tram that led up to the top of the mountain and watch the planes land at the aerodrome. But the traveller would not descend the stairs that led to the street, and when he looked down from the window at the unfamiliar city he seemed afraid.

As the days passed Jeanie began to realise that the traveller wanted only to continue his journey, but that he could not, because his coat was damaged and would no longer hold the wind. Haltingly, he tried to tell her about his home, which was somewhere far beyond the low countries and the mountains. When he spoke his whole body animated. He gestured with his hands, conjuring images in the air which he did not have the words to describe. Jeanie could only guess what he was saying, but she listened anyway, chin on her hands, just to hear the sound of his voice.

The next morning Jeanie was woken by a creaking on the ceiling above her bed. It was barely dawn, and in the half-light she imagined that it was the night of the storm all over again; but there was no rain, only a bright spring wind. Quickly she threw on her housecoat and ran to the roof.

The traveller stood with his back to the hatch, on the flat roof, with his tattered overcoat on his back and his leather case in his hand. He had his arms spread, trying to catch the wind, but it whistled through the ripped cloth and took him nowhere. When he saw her, he let his arms fall.

"It not work," he said.

Jeanie took a step to the top of the ladder, balancing half in and half out of the hatch — it was a lot scarier when she could see the long drop below.

"Come down," she said. "Come down and have something to eat."

She thought it was a silly thing to say, but the traveller followed her meekly down the ladder and back to the house, preceding her into the kitchen and taking his seat at the table with a sigh.

"You don't have to go," she said, standing nervously in the doorway. The traveller looked up, fixing his pale blue eyes on her. She couldn't tell what was going on in his mind, so she plunged on.

"I know it's not much, the bed, the house, but you can stay if you want to." Impulsively she tried to add 'I love you', but the words stuck in her throat and she did not say them.

The traveller did not reply. Instead he placed his case on the table in front of him. He rested his hands on the worn leather for a moment, then popped open the catch and lifted the lid. For a moment Jeanie thought that a warm light shone from inside the case to illuminate his face, then it was gone.

From out of the case came photographs, grainy black and white pictures with creased corners and edges smudged from long and careful handling. The first showed a woman half her age, with smiling eyes and hair tucked under an embroidered headscarf; the second, the same woman, now with a baby in her arms and the shingle boards of a house behind her back. More photographs showed strange towers with onion domes framing foggy hills, and a severe older couple on the steps of a church. Finally a single colour picture, creased down the middle, showed a young boy with tousled hair staring quizzically at the camera.

'He has his father's eyes,' Jeanie thought to herself.

Out loud she said only, "I'll help you."

Together they spread the coat out on the worn wood of the kitchen table, and Jeanie fetched needle and thread from the bedroom. She could see that darning or stitching alone would never be enough, so she cut strips of cloth from her raincoat and double-stitched them over the rips one by one. All through the night she worked, while the traveller watched her silently from the doorway.

The next morning they rose early and climbed to the roof. The sky overhead was streaked with cloud, and the wind was blowing steadily towards the east. The traveller went up first, with his case clutched in his hands, then stood with his coat flapping in the breeze.

Jeanie came up the ladder with something in her hand, a photograph of herself that she had taken from her album.

"For you," she said, holding it out.

The traveller took the photo and smiled, then tucked it into his case. With halting words he thanked her for her help, then leapt into the air, where the wind caught him and plucked him away.

"Goodbye!" he shouted, "Goodbye!".

Jeanie waved, then stood for a long while, squinting into the morning sun, as the wind carried him away into the distance. Then she pulled her coat close about her, and vanished down the stairs.

X

... is for **Xenos** (alien)

The Sandwich Thief

Have you ever seen something out of the corner of your eye that you were so sure was real it made you afraid to look back and check? Something freaky. Something so odd that you want it to be a lie? Of course you have. And of course, when you finally do dare to take that second glance, there is nothing there. You breathe a sigh of relief. You laugh to yourself to cover the embarrassment of fear.

Well, I glanced; I saw something; and when I looked back it was still there!

I was in the hallway, just rounding the corner that leads from the big rooms at the front of the house towards the bedrooms at the back. You can see through the kitchen door from there, and as I glanced in that direction I saw something standing with its back to me.

Shock! Fear! There was someone in my kitchen! I pressed my back against the hallway wall, feeling the texture of the wallpaper against my skin, and pictured what I thought I'd seen – black glossy skin, reflective, glistening like oil, not human!

My second glance was far more cautious. I pressed my hands against the wall and peeked around the corner. I looked stupid but it didn't matter, there wasn't really anyone there to see me – only there was.

I only got a glimpse, the second time; but it was enough to be sure. Something black and lithe, vanishing upwards towards the kitchen ceiling in a flash, like the after image of a snake's tail disappearing down a hole. Definitely real, definitely not human.

Not animal either. Something else.

I stayed against the wall for a long time, hardly daring to breathe, while the afternoon light slipped along the length of the hallway and shaded into evening. My fingers grew numb where they pressed against the wall, but I didn't dare to let go of the only stable thing I could reach. I jumped at every click and creak the old house made, scanning the ceiling above me in fear; but the truth was I heard nothing out of the ordinary. If I hadn't seen it, I wouldn't have known that anything was wrong.

Eventually I had to move. Hunger, cramp, the need to pee – turns out these things don't go away even when you are terrified; but where? Outside? It was a cold winter's evening, and it is a long way from my house to everywhere. I'd freeze out there – and somehow it never occurred to me to run away entirely. This was still my house. If I left now I wouldn't come back, and that was out of the question.

The bedroom then. That was easy, it was away from the kitchen, but it didn't solve anything. There was still a … something, in my kitchen. But I took stupid comfort from hiding under the bunched up covers.

Little things began to make sense: food packets not quite where I had left them; a light switched on when I was sure I'd turned it off; the unusual speed with which I'd gone through bread, pickles, dried food.

Was it making sandwiches back there?!

Eventually I found myself creeping back down the hallway with the first makeshift weapon that had come to hand – a heavy ornamental vase – clutched in my fist. Fear had bled over into anger. It was almost dark in the hall. I'd left the kitchen light on earlier and now it was the only source of light in the house. I glanced at the empty doorways of the front rooms at the end of the hall, but I didn't dare; anything could have been hiding in that darkness, and turning on the light would have given me away.

Instead I turned right, towards the kitchen.

From the doorway everything looked normal. The strip lights were on and the wooden worktops glowed with polish, but my eyes were on the ceiling, expecting to see something hideous and alien coiled on top of the cupboard tops; nothing.

Frantically I scanned the room looking for signs that I hadn't gone mad. There! The cupboard was slightly open, a torn packet of meat lay on the counter, I was sane after all!

So where had it gone?

My eyes flicked back to the ceiling tiles, and I knew. There was a space up there, a drop ceiling, wiring, an extractor fan, room to hide but no way out. I had it trapped! Assuming that it hadn't made its escape while I was hiding in the bedroom. But somehow I didn't think that it had run, any more than I had.

The discovery changed my view of the house around me. I wasn't trapped any more, it was. I had the whole house, and it only had a tiny space to cower in. I could have run, I could have called for help, but I could still have been crazy. I'd seen something from the corner of my eye. I wanted to see it clearly.

I became a hunter. I tried to think like a trapped monster. Did it know that I'd seen it? Surely it must, but its back had been turned and I'd been hiding. Was it hiding up there wondering what I knew? Was it smart? I'd interrupted its meal, was it hungry? What would it take to make it feel safe?

I entered the kitchen with exaggerated nonchalance, humming what I hoped was a happy tune. I banged cupboards, switched the kettle on, left the meat casually open on the counter as if I hadn't seen it, and then went into the sitting room, where I turned on all the lights and the TV too, making sure that anyone – or anything – could hear the clink of my mug on the table and the creak of my chair.

Then I slipped out of the room, keeping low, checking the sliver of darkened kitchen with both eyes, and planted myself in the gloom of the dining room doorway, flat on my belly; watching.

It isn't unusual for me to stay up late. I live alone – or I thought I did – with no neighbours to disturb, so the TV was plausible too. Would it come out when it thought I was still awake or would it wait? I had to count on it being hungry. I had to count on it wanting to clean up after itself.

I was willing to wait as long as it was.

The gentlest of creaks woke me. I hadn't realised till then that I'd dozed off. The chatter of the TV had faded to the muted enthusiasm of a commercial presentation; it must be very late. I'd been running on fumes for hours. The light too had dimmed – something had half-closed the sitting room door. Had I done that? or had it swung shut on its own? Either way the gloom of the hallway end was almost complete.

And something was moving in the corner of my eye.

This time I stared with both eyes and saw it for sure. Black and curling, darker than the shadows of the kitchen, I could just make it out as it lowered itself past the white fronts of the cabinets. It was large, as large as me, and my mind conjured the hundred horrific details that my eyes couldn't provide: hooks, claws, teeth, rasping edges and sucking tubes.

Which may have been why my courage failed me. All of a sudden, after hours of single minded stalking, I didn't want to confront it after all. I wanted to close my eyes, bury my face in the carpet, and pretend that I hadn't seen anything at all. I could let the night pass me by, right here, and in the morning I'd drive to town and get someone (anyone!) to come and help me.

The muffled sound of movement came from the kitchen. I heard a surreptitious rustle of plastic – the meat. Then the soft thump of a cupboard door, deliberately soft. Finally there was the distinctive pop of the fridge door opening.

For some reason, after all I'd been through that day, the thought that the creature was in my fridge rekindled my anger. Suddenly it wasn't good enough to wait till morning, I had to catch this thing now!

I let out a yell and ran. It was only a few steps from the dining room door to the kitchen, but it was already in motion, surging up towards the ceiling. This time it wasn't fast enough. I swung with the vase; lost my grip on it; grabbed a handful of something living and tugged.

It was fast, writhing in my grasp like a wildcat, but light. I pulled and we both went down, banging off the cupboards. A voice squealed. Food clattered down on my head. Limbs writhed in the darkness. Something tangled in my hair and I surged to my feet, dragging it with me. My back was to the door now and I fumbled for the light switch, a weapon, anything, sending pots and plates flying.

I reached the light switch first and snapped it on, blindingly bright. My free hand closed on the handle of a frying pan and I raised it over my head, ready to strike.

And looked down into eyes more frightened than my own.

Close up the creature looked more like a bundle of snakes than a man. What I'd taken for shell, or spines, was oily black fur, wrapped around spindly limbs that curled round my own. The limbs met in a round body the size of a football and there were eyes there, black and wild and filled with fear.

The anger blew out of me like a snuffed flame. I let the frying pan slip from my hand. I had the horrible feeling that some time during the night I'd become the monster. I'd been about to kill this thing for making a sandwich!

The creature must have sensed my slackened grip. In an instant it was out of my hands and across the floor, sending tins and bottles scattering in every direction. I made a futile snatch at one vanishing tail, but it was too quick. In a flash it was around the corner, banging through the sitting room door and out of sight.

Stupid!

I'd confronted it. I'd let it go! I'd had it pinned, trapped in the kitchen, now it could be anywhere.

I bolted for the front door. I had to get out! I dragged the door open and threw myself into the darkness; or at least I meant to. Instead I froze, hesitating on the doorstep, one hand still on the handle. If I ran, would it come after me? Were there more? If I left and came back would I still be able to find it, now that it had the whole house to hide in?

The night was cold and silent, with the taste of snow on the air. The only sound was the distant muted mumble of the television. I stared at the pale blue patch of ground illuminated by the sitting room window, imagining the creature coiling its way over the furniture, burrowing into the walls and vanishing. If I left would it get out? Would it go somewhere else? Would it be content with sandwiches and stolen milk? Would it grow to like me? Would it remember my violence and decide to attack the next time it saw a human being?

Slowly I turned around, hardly believing what I was doing, and stepped back into the house. I closed the door behind me and pressed my back against it, scanning the darkness, taking big breaths of inside air. I couldn't see anything, but I knew it was there, somewhere.

Could I do this? I had to. Who else but me? Somehow I couldn't imagine bringing anyone else into this now. It was my house, and my problem, and I'd just have to find a way to deal with it – or live with it. Besides, it had seen me too. It wasn't going to let me go, and I couldn't let it go. If it hid, I'd catch it, and then we'd see.

I took a breath, and headed back into the darkness.

Y

... is for **Yearning**

Seaweed Memories

Ailsa rose early, and went down to the shore to gather seaweed memories. They were spread out along the grey rocks where the sea had left them — green, brown, black, purple, even a few red ones spread out on the sand.

The green were the commonplace memories: shopping lists and school lessons, what someone ate the day before, conversations on the train. The brown memories showed the signs of age, they were the recollections of childhoods at the coast, or hard winters in the hills; old dead friends, and houses no longer lived in. Black and purple were close-held things, secret and private memories that should never have been lost. The red were the rarest, memories of violence and murder — Ailsa had no interest in them.

Carefully she peeled the drying memories off the rocks and held them up to the morning sun. To her practiced eye the curlicues and dapples on the surface were as easy to read as a music score. Here a little boy's memories of ice cream on the beach; here an old woman's summer day before the war; here a guilty dalliance with a beautiful girl, cut off abruptly where the sharp rocks had cut it in two. Some memories came away as bright and gay as summer ribbons, others crumbled to dust as they left the rocks.

Ailsa stacked the memories in her basket, pressing them flat between sheets of cotton as she moved her way along the shore. She whistled nervously to herself as she worked. To the east the sun rose higher over the green-blue sea, trailing flocks of seagulls.

Eventually the sound of voices broke the silence. Footsteps thudded on the path that led down from the village, and Ailsa heard Morag's raucous laughter; Fiona's scandalised whispering. The rest of the girls were coming to start the day's harvest.

Ailsa stopped and stretched her back, which was sore from stooping. She had been at work for two hours already. Absent-mindedly she plucked one last yellowing kelp frond from the sand, then hurried up the beach with her basket clutched in her arms.

She passed the others on the trail, mouthing good mornings and avoiding their eyes. No one would be surprised at her early rising, or her early leaving – it was well known that she helped the Minister up at the manse with the schooling of the children. Still, she preferred to avoid their questions.

Only Angus stopped, passing by on his way to the boats. He was wearing a rough-knit sweater, and he had his hands tucked in his pockets. He smiled at her, and she was forced to stop, resting the basket on her hip.

"I, eh, cut my beard," he said.

"Aye, so you did."

"Right, aye ..." he made to step forward but bumped into the basket, which had somehow ended up between them.

"I'd best get on," she said, and headed on up the hill.

Safely ensconced in the gloom of the manse, Ailsa placed her basket on the old leather top of the Minister's desk, and uncovered the fronds inside. In theory all the memories gathered on the shore went up to the factory, where they were dried, pressed, and shipped to the mainland for reuse. In the big cities, island memories were cut up for newspaper articles, pasted wholesale into advertising jingles and magazine horoscopes. The choicest reminiscences were sold to authors and journalists, or supplied to politicians in need of stirring similes.

The nastiest memories were shredded for use in legal arguments and fortune cookies, but there were always those willing to sell the red fronds under the table. Ailsa knew that some of the village girls slipped the red memories to their men before their baskets were weighed in, but she had no interest in that trade. Her own load would go to the mill when she was done in the manse, unless ...

Carefully she slipped certain memories — ones that she had marked by touch with a folded corner — out of her basket and held them up to the light, teasing her way through them by touch and eye. The first bore the faint scent of roses — a trip to the park on a late summer's day, hand in hand; but it was a woman's memories, not what she wanted. The second came from a boat at sea. It was the memory of a storm, of a man lashed to a tiller hoping to steer a way home, and it made her heart race, but it was not her man.

She glanced at the half-closed door behind her to make sure that the Minister had not come in, and then slipped the notebook out from the pocket of her skirt. Between its pages she had hidden seven browning fronds, the real reason that she went down to the beach so early every morning.

She had found the first of them when she was still a girl, following her mother down to the beach on a working day. She had wandered away from the gang of busy women and found a scrap of memory washed up on the sand. For some reason it had spoken to her, and instead of dropping it in her mother's basket she had hidden it in her blouse and taken it home.

Tucked up in her loft bed, she had laboriously deciphered the memory of a man setting out on a journey. He was leaving home, crossing the hills on his way to the sea, not knowing if he would come back again. Something about the memory captivated her. She didn't even know the man's name, but she kept it hidden away.

Years later, when she had started seaweed collecting on her own, she had found another. She had known it as soon as she had plucked it from the rock, it had his scent, his aura. This time, working as part of a gang, all freshly out of school, she had been forced to hide the memory under her skirt to keep it from the communal basket – everyone had heard the gossip about the red-smugglers from their parents.

Since then she had managed to piece together seven steps in the stranger's story. From that first day in the hills he had travelled to the coast – the memory of his first sight of the sea had been the third she had found – and begun a life on the sea. Though no memory ever named the port he sailed from, she had convinced herself that it couldn't be far away; maybe just across the sound towards the mainland, nestled amongst the distant blue hills she could see from the manse window.

The fourth memory was the most precious of all. It was a purple one, and she was sure it was only an echo of something he treasured. In it, the man stood by the tiller of his boat, guiding it through the crowded waters of an island harbour. As his gaze slid across the busy dockside it came to rest on a passing girl, a girl that caught his heart and took his breath away. It was only the briefest of glances, but it stuck with him – and surely the port he was in looked like Balhoolie down at the end of the island where they shipped the memories out; and surely the girl he'd seen had worn the same dress she'd worn the day the new pier opened, and had her hair, and her colouring.

In her daydreams she'd imagined him coming back for her in a hundred different ways: knocking on her mother's door, asking after her at the manse, sweeping her in his arms as she worked on the sands; but the war had come instead.

The war had taken a few of the menfolk from the island, those that didn't work on the memory shipments, but many more from the mainland. The fifth and sixth memories that Ailsa had found, black and spiky and close together, showed that her man had gone to war with the rest of them, taking his boat up north to the naval yards, then out east to the fighting. She'd almost fainted in fear when she'd found them; and had nearly told her mother everything. Instead she'd joined the wives who combed the papers for news of their husbands, hoping not to see news of brave sailors drowned.

Then, only weeks ago, the seventh memory, the one that scared her most. A storm, a heaving sea, a ship under fire. It was a desperate memory, a violent one, the kind of memory left by men who died at sea.

She'd been up before dawn and down at the beach every day since then, hoping to find a memory of his survival; but so far she'd found nothing.

She shut the notebook with a sigh, and let it fall to the table. She was out of time. She could hear the Minister on the path outside, and the ruckus of the children. Quickly she began to pack the memories back into her basket, pushing them down under their layers of cloth.

As she rooted around the basket her hand brushed against the yellow kelp she picked up as she left the beach, and she felt a thrill that raised the fine hairs on her arm. There was something there, something about that memory …

It was his.

Hesitantly she lifted the frond from the basket, feeling the slippery smoothness of its surface. This memory was new, fresh, full of life; a foam-light echo of the happiest of thoughts. In the light that shone through the half open window it glowed like cut horn, or amber.

With trembling fingers she teased images from the golden surface: the sea, rolling and green, the chug of an engine, a boat, the smell of fresh spray on the wind. He was standing on the deck, watching the sun roll over the sea, trailing seagulls. The boards rolled easily under his feet, and he took a deep excited breath. His thoughts were full of the girl on the pier he had seen years before — full of her!

The Minister was at the door, but she was too deep in the memory to care. Her man was guiding his boat towards an island that peeked, grey-green, above the surging sea. Her island! Today! He was coming for her!

The Minister came through the door stamping his feet, and was almost bowled over as Ailsa ran past him, dress flapping, face grinning, basket upturned on the floor.

"Ailsa!" he called, "it's time for the school!"

But she was already on the path and running towards the sea, all else forgotten.

Z

… is for **Zugzwang** (to be compelled to do something disadvantageous to yourself)

The Detective

On Friday morning, at 10:15 am, John Finn receives a phone call on the antique dial phone that sits on his office desk.

"Hello?" He answers the phone gruffly, not bothering to introduce himself, because he was not expecting a call, and the sound of the phone has annoyed him. His query is answered by near silence. He can hear someone breathing short anxious breaths. It sounds to him like someone is working up the courage to speak.

"Hello?" He puts a little more force into the word, "who's there?"

"Is that Detective Finn? Are you the John Finn Detective Agency?"

The question makes John Finn hesitate. Is he John Finn, detective? Of course he is. Isn't he sitting at a desk in a room with 'Detective Agency' stencilled in gold letters on the door? He is.

"Yes, that's me."

The voice on the other end of the line is male, but the connection is poor, so Finn can't be sure if he recognises it or not.

"I need you to investigate a murder," says the voice.

"A murder? That's for the police, not me."

"Call it a missing person case then."

"A missing person I can do, but if it turns out there's a

death involved I'll have to call the cops in anyway. Now, I'll need some details." As he speaks Finn pulls open the desk drawer in search of something to write on. Instantly notebooks start to pour out, like popcorn emerging from a popcorn maker. He tries to close the drawer, but it won't close, and he still needs a notebook, but every time he makes a grab for one, it skitters away from his grasp.

While Finn struggles to provide himself a notebook and a pen, the voice explains that the missing person is a close friend, a relation, or a vital business colleague – perhaps all three, Finn isn't quite sure. This man, normally a dependable (if humdrum) insurance agent, appears to have vanished from the face of the earth, and the voice wants Finn to find him.

"You got an address there?"

"One hundred and fifty three, Oakland Avenue, apartment 13."

"I know it," Finn replies, although for a moment he can't actually picture Oakland Avenue, imagining instead the house in which he grew up, which was not on Oakland Avenue, or indeed, even in the same city.

Flustered, Finn looks at his notes – which he has scrawled on the back of a parking ticket – and realises that he has managed to miss the missing person's name. Rather than admit this blunder to his unknown client, he asks, "How can I reach you?"

"I'll call you," the voice says, and the line goes dead.

Later, Finn finds himself on Oakland Avenue. It is a row of high, narrow, post-war houses, but for some reason the entrance to number 153 has been surrounded with thick masses of fuchsia, so that the buildings to either side are concealed behind a wall of pink and purple blossoms. Walking between them he is reminded of a house he'd once owned up in the west side, and is unsurprised when the door opens into the familiar hallway of his house, with the communal stair in front of him, and a bank of letterboxes on the left. Except, of course, his old house didn't have a bank of letterboxes, or a communal stairway. This isn't his home after all, but an entirely different building.

Apartment 13 is on the third floor. The corridor is dark and narrow, with three brown doors and a dirty skylight overhead. Finn bangs on the door of number 13 with a closed fist, putting his ear to the wood between knocks to see if he can hear anyone moving. Unopened letters and rolled-up newspapers are piled up around his feet in something like a snowdrift, and for a moment Finn loses his footing and thinks that he is going to slide all the way down this mountain of paper; but he does not.

The door on the other side of the hallway opens a crack, and an old woman peers out at Finn past the heavy chain.

"Hey," Finn says, heading over, "you know the guy who lives in 13?"

"Mr Finn?".

Finn starts in surprise. "How did you know my name?"

The old lady looks at him like he's mad, and explains that her missing neighbour is called Mick Finn.

"Sounds like a fake name," Finn grunts. As soon as the words are out of his mouth he thinks that it was an odd thing to say, because his own initials are actually M.J.F, the M standing for Michael, a first name he's never actually liked.

He leans into the door, making sure that his foot will be in the way when the woman tries to close it, and grills her about the missing man. He learns that Mick Finn is a nice young man, and that she (Mrs Sito), can always rely on him to help her with her garbage; and that she hasn't seen him in at least five days now; and that she is really quite worried about him.

"You ask a lot of questions," she says, when her monologue finally comes to a stop, "just like that other guy."

"What other guy?" Finn asks, thinking that maybe he has gotten a lead on his elusive client.

"I got a card here." Mrs Sito fishes around behind the door and produces a small rectangle of paper. It has writing on it, but for some reason Finn can't seem to read it. Luckily Mrs Sito reads it herself, pronouncing each word with exaggerated care, "Doctor James Minwell, Cherry Tree Institute. He was round here asking questions, same as you."

Later, Finn finds himself outside the Cherry Tree Institute, which is an anonymous glass and steel medical building on the north side of town. There is a billboard-shaped sign outside, but Finn can't see it because of the masses of sunflowers that have been planted all across the lawn. The sunflowers are taller than his head, and he has to push his way through them with both hands to go towards the building. This takes a long time, possibly hours, in which the same patch of sunflowers blocks his way repeatedly, as if he is going in circles. Only when Finn reminds himself that he is a detective on an important case does he stumble through the Institute's front door; by which time he is breathing heavily and covered in pollen.

Doctor Minwell turns out to be a middle aged man with crazy Einstein hair and an office hip deep in paper. He offers Finn the only clear chair and then perches himself on the edge of his desk.

"You are looking for Mick, Mr …"

"Finn," says Finn.

"That's a co-incidence." Finn makes a noise of agreement, but he's distracted, because he has somehow become entangled in the chair he's sitting on, and can't move his feet. He tries to tug one of his legs free, but the chair is like an immovable object, and when he feels around under the seat to see what has trapped him, his hand gets stuck as well.

"I'm very worried about Mick," the Doctor says, as if

unaware of Finn's difficulties. "I think something very bad may have happened to him."

"What sort of thing?" Finn asks. He has managed to free his right leg, but he still has one foot and one hand stuck under the chair.

"That's difficult to explain." The Doctor falls silent for a while, and Finn considers, and then dismisses, the possibility that he was the caller at 10:15 am.

Finn tries a different tack. "What is your relationship with Mr Finn?"

"I am his physician."

"This doesn't look like a regular doctor's office to me, Doctor." Finn is finally free of the chair, and can't understand how he came to be trapped in the first place, so he paces as he talks, picking his way around the doctor's papers.

"Ahh yes." The doctor has very wide watery eyes, and he blinks them constantly while he is speaking. "I am a specialist. But I don't know if I really should be discussing this with you."

"I am just trying to find Mick," Finn assures him.

"And you are sure that you are a real detective?"

"Of course I am. I have an office with 'Detective Agency' written on the door."

The doctor appears to accept this argument without question, and launches into a case history.

"Mick has been my patient for some time, but he is a friend as well, and I'm really quite worried about him. You see for some time he has been going ... away, and I'm concerned that this time it might be permanent."

"Away? What do you mean Doc?"

"Away ... he vanishes. He closes his eyes, and then, he's just not there any more. It's like he's died, except that he comes back."

Finn tries to make sense of what the doctor is saying, but there is a lot he doesn't understand. He takes out a school notebook in which it appears he has written notes, and stares at the scrawl as if it will help. Finally he says, "Closes his eyes? What, you mean like blinking?"

The doctor shakes his head, "No, he closes his eyes, and then keeps them closed, and then he … isn't there any more." He shrugs his shoulders, eloquently conveying his confusion. Finn tries to imagine what it would look like, or feel like, to close one's eyes and keep them closed, but he can't. The idea of people simply disappearing from the world, and then coming back, is unsettling too. It sounds a lot like dying.

"So you think that Mick might have closed his eyes for too long and what, gone poof?" He makes a hand gesture.

"Yes, exactly that. When he didn't come to his appointments I got worried, but I didn't really know what to do. I called his office but they hadn't seen him either. I thought about contacting the police, but how would I explain?

"There is one thing though."

"Oh?"

The doctor fumbles in his desk drawers while Finn peers over his shoulder, and then pulls out a latch key. It is brass, with a little rubber ring around the fat end, and a metal keyring attached.

"Is that what I think it is Doc?"

"Yes, Mick gave me his door-key, just about a month ago. He was very worried. He said it was in case of emergencies, but I haven't dared to use it."

"You can give it to me."

"No, no, I better come with you."

Later, Finn finds himself back in the apartment building corridor, with Doctor Minwell at his side. The doctor fumbles with the key, then pushes open the door to reveal the entrance of a narrow apartment, which is built shotgun style — a series of rooms opening off a single passageway. A dial clock is hanging on the wall, showing that the time is 10:15.

The two of them enter a crowded sitting room, one end of which has been set up as a home office, with an antique writing table crammed under a rack of shelves. The lowest shelf is filled with classic hardboiled fiction; Raymond Chandler and Dashiell Hammett, bracketed by James M. Cain.

Above the detective books a battered leather briefcase is sitting on its side, with the handle and lock facing the room. On the top of the case the initials M.J.F have been embossed in scuffed gold.

"What the hell!" Finn exclaims, yanking the case from the shelf, "these are my initials!"

"Really? Well I suppose Mick's full name is Michael John Finn ..."

Finn feels an enormous sense of dislocation, as if he might faint. That is *his* full name, and this is *his* briefcase, and — he realises — this is *his* apartment. The walls of the sitting room pulse in and out of focus, and he is struck with the sudden nonsensical conviction that he is not, in fact, a detective, but is actually an insurance agent. For a horrible moment nothing makes any sense, and he thinks that things are falling apart.

He is brought abruptly back to his senses when Minwell grabs him by the shoulders.

"My god man! You were just like him! You closed your eyes and you began vanishing!"

Finn collapses heavily into a nearby chair, clutching the briefcase to his chest like a life preserver. "What does it mean, Doc? Is this thing catching? Am I going to die?"

The doctor pulls a spiral notebook from his pocket and

perches on the edge of Finn's desk. "Tell me how you feel," the doctor says. "What did you experience when your eyes were closed?"

Finn has no desire to discuss the horrible sensation of being an insurance agent instead of a detective, or the feeling that nothing here is real, so instead of answering he jumps out of the chair and sets about Mick Finn's papers in a frenzy. Ransacking the drawers and shelves he piles up a stack of photo albums and diaries, which he dumps on the coffee table.

The photo albums are full of cameo pictures of Finn's mother, father, and sister, as well as another man who looks exactly like Finn. One full page photo shows a picnic that Finn remembers clearly from his childhood, taken by the side of a river. His mother is in the foreground, while his paternal grandmother, who was called Luna, perches primly on a camp stool in the background. Once again he feels dizzy and confused, and the doctor hops off the edge of the table, no doubt about to tell him that he is fading away again, so he snaps the album shut and turns to the diaries.

"Look at this," he says to Minwell.

The diaries are filled with close packed writing. Micky Finn has been scrawling his experiences after each attack, using a blue ball-point pen. Certain words are repeated over and over, but Finn can't make them out.

"What does this say?" he points the words out to the doctor, "and this?"

Minwell peers closer. "Sleep. Dream. I don't know what those words mean, do you?"

"No!" Finn shouts, but he has a horrible feeling that he does know what they mean.

He jumps up from his chair, frantic, upsetting the coffee table in the process. He crashes his way from room to room with the doctor in pursuit, knocking over furniture, breaking ornaments, and flinging open cupboards, as if searching for something.

"Mr Finn!" The doctor tries to reason with him, grabbing hold of his arm, "Control yourself!"

"No!" Finn shouts again, "I need to get out of here. I need to get back to where this all started! The man on the phone, I need to find the man on the phone!" In his desperation he shoves the doctor against the wall, sending books and ornaments showering down to the floor. The apartment is now literally disintegrating, the walls and floors separating from one another. "I need to go back!"

Now Finn is in his office, sitting in his chair. The antique phone is positioned to his right at a slight angle, so that it is easy to pick up, while the school notebook is on the left. The flip down clock next to the phone shows 10:15.

The glass panel office door opens and Doctor Minwell enters, but Finn ignores him, because he is waiting for the phone to ring. When it does, he snatches the handset from the cradle and answers, "Hello?"

For a moment all he can hear is the sound of breathing, and then the voice says, "Is that Detective Finn? Are you the John Finn Detective Agency?" This time Finn recognises the voice on the other end of the line as his own, and he understands why John Finn vanishes when his eyes are closed, and why no one in this world has heard of dreaming.

"No," he says, "this is not a detective agency. I am not a detective, I am an insurance agent."

Then he closes his eyes, and wakes up.

About the Author

I usually describe myself as an artist, a programmer, a reader, and a writer, perhaps in that order. I have written short stories (and novels) of countless types since I was old enough to hold a pencil – many are very embarrassing, some of the others are here. I have also written and published a number of Roleplaying Games; if you are interested you can check out my Website.

I live in a garret (really a top-floor flat, but a garret sounds a lot more romantic) in Edinburgh with my wife Victoria, 2 cats, and lots of reptiles, a number of which also appear in this book in various ways.

You can find me online at:

- Facebook – www.facebook.com/dmskdonachie
- Website – www.teuton.org/~stranger
- Grophland – www.grophland.com

If you enjoyed The Night Alphabet then a review on its Amazon page would be very much appreciated!

28169418R00100

Printed in Great Britain
by Amazon